THE INCREDIBLE RESCUES

Books by Ed Dunlop

The Young Refugees

Escape to Liechtenstein

The Search for the Silver Eagle

The Incredible Rescues

THE INCREDIBLE RESCUES

THE YOUNG REFUGEES

ED DUNLOP

Greenville, South Carolina

Library of Congress Cataloging-in-Publication Data
Dunlop, Ed, 1955-
The incredible rescues / by Ed Dunlop ; [illustrated by Tom Halverson].—Rev. ed.
p. cm.—(The young refugees ; bk. 3)
Summary: Fourteen-year-old Hans and his younger sister Gretchen trust in the Lord as they help Swedish diplomat Raoul Wallenberg save Jews from the Nazis in Budapest, Hungary, during the closing days of World War II.
ISBN 1-59166-012-2 (Perfect bound paperback : alk. paper)
1. Wallenberg, Raoul, 1912-1947--Juvenile fiction. 2. World War, 1939-1945—Jews—Rescue—Hungary—Budapest—Juvenile fiction. [1. Wallenberg, Raoul, 1912-1947—Fiction. 2. World War, 1939-1945—Jews—Rescue—Fiction. 3. Holocaust, Jewish (1939-1945)—Hungary—Fiction. 4. Righteous Gentiles in the Holocaust—Fiction. 5. Brothers and sisters—Fiction. 6. Christian life—Fiction.] I. Halverson, Tom, ill. II. Title II. Series: Dunlop, Ed, 1955- , Young refugees ; bk. 3.
PZ7.D92135In 2004
[Fic]—dc22

2003021166

Designed by Micah Ellis
Illustrated by Tom Halverson
Composited by Melissa Matos

Greenville, SC 29614

Printed in the United States of America

ISBN 1-59166-012-2
15 14 13 12 11 10 9 8 7 6 5 4 3 2 1

"And whosoever will be chief among you, let him be your servant: even as the Son of man came not to be ministered unto, but to minister, and to give his life a ransom for many."
Matthew 20:27–28

Contents

Introduction

In the last months of World War II, most of Europe was *Judenfrei*—free of Jews. Karl Adolf Eichmann and his death trains were transporting Jewish men, women, and children to Auschwitz and other death camps at the rate of twelve thousand per day. The bodies of these innocent people were buried in mass graves in the forests surrounding the camps.

By the summer of 1944, the only large remaining Jewish population lived in the war-torn land of Hungary, with nearly half a million Jews residing in the capital, Budapest. The president of the United States, Franklin Delano Roosevelt, formed the War Refugee Board in a desperate attempt to save a remnant of the Jewish people. The president's staff searched for a volunteer to attempt a rescue of the Budapest Jews, but nobody was willing to undertake such a dangerous mission. Finally, someone suggested the name of a young Swedish businessman, Raoul Wallenberg. The thirty-one-year-old man accepted the mission eagerly.

After taking the position of Second Secretary of the Swedish Legation in Hungary, Wallenberg threw himself wholeheartedly into the work of rescuing the Jewish people. In one incredible rescue after another, Wallenberg and his staff saved thousands upon thousands of Jews from death at the hands of the Nazis. Wallenberg had the heart of a servant. This book is written as a tribute to a courageous, unselfish man who proved once and for all that even during the darkest of times, one person can make a difference.

CHAPTER ONE

THE DEATH TRAINS

Three black locomotives sat idling on the tracks beside the Jozsefvarosi freight station on the eastern outskirts of Budapest, Hungary. The iron rails hummed with the vibrations from their powerful engines. A light rain drizzled down, adding to the gloom and misery of the cold October morning.

"Move along, you dirty Jews!" a Nazi soldier screamed, swinging his rifle to strike a young Jewish man across the back. "*Schnell machen!* Faster. Faster!"

Harsh voices echoed across the freight yard as black-booted Nazi officers rolled back the rusty doors of the waiting cattle cars. German soldiers used curses and rifle butts to drive a huge mass of frightened, bewildered people across the platform toward the train. The soldiers wore red and black armbands displaying the swastika of the Third Reich; their captives each wore a yellow, six-pointed star prominently displayed over their left breast. Guards with automatic rifles stood watch on top of the cattle cars.

Gretchen moved closer to her brother, Hans. Their position on top of an old freight wagon at the far end of the platform afforded them a clear view of the entire proceedings. "They're being led like sheep, aren't they?" Gretchen said quietly. "Thousands of frightened sheep, huddled together, simply going wherever they are led. Hans, why don't they fight back? Why don't they run away?"

Hans sighed. "They've given up hope, Gretchen. I suppose they've been told so many times that they are worthless that they've started believing it. Besides, what good is it to fight when the soldiers have automatic rifles? Those who resist would simply be shot on the spot."

Gretchen clutched his hand. "Isn't this a train headed for Auschwitz—the death camp?"

Hans nodded.

Gretchen began to sob. The Nazis had already taken the life of their mother while they lived in Austria. Hans and Gretchen had barely escaped Austria, and now they were witnessing Nazi hatred in the streets of Budapest. But this was even more cruel and heartless than anything they had yet seen. "Then these people will all be killed! Hans, look at all the children in the crowd. Isn't there something we can do?"

Hans swallowed hard and squeezed his sister's hand.

They watched helplessly as the soldiers loaded the first cattle car, shoving and cursing until there was not room for another person. When the car was crammed to capacity, a soldier placed a single loaf of bread and a bucket of water on the floor and then rolled the door closed with a loud thud. A second soldier locked it.

Hans and Gretchen continued to watch in agonized silence as the loading progressed. A group of bystanders began to form. As the people watched, the soldiers continued to herd the silent Jewish families toward the second and third cars. They cursed and shouted, kicking with a polished boot or striking out with a rifle whenever a straggler moved too slowly.

An old man hesitated at the edge of the platform, looking for someone to help him step across the empty space to the cattle car. With a trembling hand he attempted to adjust his glasses, but they slipped from his grasp and fell to the platform. A young boy rushed forward to retrieve the glasses, but a soldier leaped ahead of him, smashed the glasses under the heel of his boot, and then used his rifle to knock the old man across to the floor of the car. There was no protest, no attempt to escape. A few soldiers with their guns were in control of the thousands of helpless people.

A timid mother with a baby and two young children struggled to step across to the cattle car. Her oldest child, a little girl four years of age, screamed with fear and turned to run away. A soldier picked the child up and hurled her into the car. Gretchen winced.

Hans's heart was heavy as he watched the loading continue. How could the Nazis be so heartless? How could they sentence these innocent people to death, simply because they were Jewish? Old men, women, little children—it made no difference to the Nazis. The German people had believed Hitler's lies, and now hatred was so strong that it could motivate an otherwise civilized people to kill innocent men, women, and children. Among the helpless group were those dressed in well-made and expensive clothing. They were, no doubt, at one time business owners, doctors, or lawyers.

"They're packing the people in so tightly they can't even sit down." Gretchen was angry. "They loaded eighty-seven people into that one car." Her voice rose to a shrill scream. "Eighty-seven people, Hans! With just one loaf of bread and a bucket of water!"

Hans glanced at her and then back at the train. "There's nothing we can do, Gretchen. Please keep your voice down."

"How long will the trip take?"

Hans paused. "About a week."

"Will they stop to give these people food or water?"

Hans's lips became a thin, hard line. "Not a chance."

Gretchen dug her fingers into his arm. "Hans, somebody has to do something. The Nazis have no right to kill these people just because they're Jewish!"

Hans tried to quiet her. "Gretchen, you must not draw attention to us," he whispered.

She raised a tear-stained face to look at him. "But look at those people, Hans. Some of them are so weak now that they can hardly stand, and many of them will be dead before they even get to Auschwitz. Isn't there something we can do?"

Hans shook his head grimly. "There's nothing to do, Gretchen."

A man in the elite black-uniformed *Schutzstaffel*—the SS guard—came striding across the wooden platform toward the freight wagon. "You there," he called, gesturing toward them with his Mauser automatic. "What are you doing here?" The officer was so close that Hans could see the white death's head on the shiny black visor of his hat.

Fear swept over Hans. "W-We're just w-watching, Herr Captain," he stammered.

"Move out of here!" the Nazi barked. "*Mach schnell!* Before I decide to put you on the train with those dirty Jews."

Hans seized his sister by the arm and moved toward the edge of the wagon. "*Ja,* we're going, Herr Captain. Come on, Gretchen."

The officer stood watching as Hans and Gretchen quickly climbed down from the freight wagon and walked across the platform toward the end of the freight depot. When they were safely behind the building, Hans stopped and turned toward the street. "Come on, Gretchen, let's go home."

Gretchen shook her head. "*Nein,* we have to stay, Hans," she argued. "Maybe there's nothing we can do for these people, but I need to stay and watch. As horrible as it is, we can't just walk away as if nothing is happening."

"We don't dare go back to the platform," Hans replied. "You heard what that officer told us." The cold rain began to fall faster, and Hans pulled the collar of his coat up against his neck.

"Maybe we can watch from a safer place."

Hans thought for a moment. "There's an old steel foundry across the tracks," he said. "We can cross behind the train and watch from there. This is the side with all the action, but we'll be able to see at least a little of what's going on."

Walking swiftly, Hans and Gretchen passed behind the freight depot, hurried down the block, and crossed the tracks behind the train. A railroad spur split off from the main line and snaked its way behind a rough wooden fence to terminate at the abandoned foundry building. Hans and Gretchen followed the tracks.

Two abandoned boxcars sat forlornly on the spur while various pieces of scrap steel and old equipment lay rusting in the waist-high weeds. A huge, cylindrical tank lay on its side. Large sections were rusted away, and Hans peered inside. Broken pallets and scraps of wood littered the ground beneath the tank.

Gretchen crouched in the weeds behind the fence to look through a crack between the planks. "Over here, Hans," she called softly. "I can see the train from here."

The railroad cars obscured most of their view. However, they could see enough through the spaces between the cars to tell that the platform was nearly empty. Most of the condemned Jews had been loaded, and the remaining two or three hundred were now being herded into the last cars. Hans sighed. The train was almost ready to roll.

Gretchen pulled at his sleeve. "Look, Hans. What's that fellow doing?"

Hans twisted around and peered through the crack in the direction that Gretchen pointed. As he watched, a figure slipped furtively along the side of the cattle cars. Crouching low, the man paused at the forward end of each car, glanced upward toward the soldiers on the roof, and hurried across to the next car.

"What's he doing?" Gretchen repeated.

"I don't know," Hans replied, "but it looks like he's up to something, doesn't it?"

"He's carrying a pipe or some sort of tool."

"I wonder what he plans to do with it." As Hans spoke, the shadowy figure rose to his feet beside the third car from the front. Hans and Gretchen could now see that he was a young man about Hans's age.

The youth glanced up quickly, then stepped away from the side of the train and swung the heavy pipe against the locked door. "He's trying to smash the lock!" Hans gasped in astonishment.

"Hans, they'll kill him," Gretchen breathed.

The boy swung the pipe twice more and then dropped it beside the tracks. Bracing his feet in the gravel, he pushed with all his strength. The cattle car door rolled slowly to one side. "He got it open," Hans exclaimed.

"Run," the boy urged the car's occupants, who stood blinking against the brightness. "Run for your lives! They're going to kill you! Run!"

The boy stooped, picked up his pipe, and ran to the next car. Within seconds, he had managed to open that door as well. "Run," he said urgently.

Two young women jumped from the second car to land sprawling in the gravel. They leaped to their feet and sprinted into the woods beyond the foundry. The sight spurred the others to action, and they poured from the two open doors.

A guard atop the train noticed the escaping prisoners. "Halt!" he screamed, throwing his Mauser to his shoulder. He pelted the scattering group with automatic weapon fire. A number of escapees fell to the ground. The three other guards atop the train spun around and fired a volley of shots. More people fell.

The escape attempt was over almost before it had started. Many of the Jews not hit by gunfire turned and raced back to the cattle car, desperate in their attempts to scramble back inside. Others simply raised their hands over their heads and walked back.

The youth with the pipe was attempting to open the door on the third car when he heard the chatter of the automatic weapons. He dropped his pipe and dashed across the gravel, heading straight for the fence where Hans and Gretchen were hiding. A trail of bullets swept the ground just behind him, but he dodged and twisted as he raced frantically for the refuge of the fence. Suddenly, with a cry of agony, he fell to the ground less than five meters from the end of the fence.

Hans leaped to his feet, but Gretchen seized his sleeve. "Hans, what are you doing?" she cried.

"We can't just let them kill him!" Hans shouted. "I have to help him."

"Hans, they'll shoot you!" Gretchen screamed, but her brother had already pulled free of her grasp. He dashed around the end of the fence.

Somehow the youth had crawled to the end of the fence. Hans seized him by both wrists and dragged him around the corner.

"Leave me," the youth ordered. "Get out of here. They'll kill you!"

"I'll help you," Hans replied. "You're hurt." He leaned over, lifted the other boy in his arms, and ran along the backside of the fence.

"Just leave me here," the stranger insisted. "Run for your life."

"We'll not leave you to die," Hans whispered fiercely.

"Inside that big tank, Hans," Gretchen called. "It's the only place to hide." She scrambled through one of the openings in the side of the tank.

Hans raced after her. As he passed a broken section in the fence, he glanced toward the train. Two Nazi soldiers were scrambling down from the roof of the cattle cars.

CHAPTER TWO
MIKLÖS TOTH

Fear stabbed at Hans's heart as he realized that the two Nazi soldiers were coming to search for them. It would take mere seconds for them to round the corner of the fence, and then it would be over.

Hans carried the injured youth to a gaping hole in the side of the tank and set him down. Frantically, he ducked through the opening and then, gripping the stranger by the wrists, dragged him inside.

Gretchen appeared at his side. "Here," she whispered, "cover him with this." She thrust a large piece of rotting tarpaulin into his hands. Hans threw the tarp over the injured boy, then seized a broken, wooden pallet, and laid it over the tarp to help camouflage the hiding place.

He spun around to see Gretchen scoot under a large, flat section of iron sheeting. He dropped to his belly and crawled in after her. They lay absolutely still, hardly daring to breathe.

"Where are—" Gretchen whispered, but Hans clapped a hand over her mouth.

Placing his lips right against her ear he whispered, "Don't move." Shots rang out. A black boot suddenly appeared at the edge of the tank.

"They're in here," a gruff voice barked in German. "They didn't have time to get any farther."

"I hit the first *knabe,*" a second voice replied. "I know I did."

"We'll find them," the first voice replied. "But hurry! The train won't wait."

The boot disappeared from view. A board broke with a loud crack, and Hans knew that the two soldiers had entered the tank. *Help us, Lord!* he prayed desperately. If the soldiers discovered their hiding place, the three of them would be shot on the spot.

One of the soldiers cursed. "It sure is dark in here."

"We'll find them."

Hans slowly reached out and touched Gretchen. She was trembling. *Lord, please help us!* he prayed again.

The train whistle blasted suddenly and one of the soldiers cursed again. "They're leaving!"

"Find the kids," the other ordered. "We know they're in here."

"I'm not staying," the first soldier said flatly. "If we miss that train, Dannecker will have our heads."

"It'll just take a minute," the other soldier growled. "We'll still catch the train."

"I'm not taking that chance." The sound of receding footsteps told Hans that the man had run back to the train. The other soldier cursed again.

Hans lay silently. He listened intently, but heard only the distant rumble of the locomotive engines. The crash of metal on metal reverberated across the train yard as the cattle car couplings pulled against each other. The train was pulling out of the station. Holding his breath, Hans backed out of his hiding place and crawled to the opening in the side of the tank.

The death train was chugging out of the station, and the two Nazi soldiers were not in sight. Hans breathed a long sigh of relief and turned to his sister. "Let's find a better hiding place just in case someone at the depot saw what happened," he whispered.

Hans lifted the broken pallet to one side and pulled back the tarp. "How badly are you hurt?" he asked the injured boy.

"It's just my foot," the other answered. "Hurry. There isn't time to look at it now."

"Weren't you hit anywhere else?" Hans asked in surprise.

"I don't think so," the boy answered. "But hurry! We must get out of here. I know a good place inside the foundry. Can you help me get to it?" He crawled through the opening in the side of the tank. Hans and Gretchen followed.

The injured youth pulled himself upright using the tank for support. Blood dripped from his right shoe to form a little puddle on the ground. "I'll lean on you," he said to Hans, "and you can help me walk. I know a way to get inside the building."

"Why don't I carry you?" Hans suggested. "It'll be faster."

The boy shrugged as he eyed Hans's frame. "Suit yourself. You did it once already."

Hans stooped and lifted the other boy in his arms, noting with surprise how light he was. With Gretchen at his heels, he headed for the side of the foundry building. "Go to the third door," the stranger instructed. "I'll show you how to get in."

They reached the third door safely. "Set me down," the boy urged Hans. He grimaced and sucked in his breath as the injured foot struck the ground. Gingerly, he tried walking but opted to use only his good foot.

The boy looked in every direction and gripped the doorknob with both hands. He pulled hard to one side, and the door popped open. "The latch doesn't go far enough into the door frame," he explained. "Let's get inside."

Hans lifted him again. "Gretchen, take my hat," he suggested, "and hold it under his foot so we don't leave a trail of blood."

"Upstairs to the second floor," the boy directed when they were safely inside. "There's a small closet that we can lock from the inside. It'll be a safe place to hide for the next hour or so. It even has a window, so we will have light."

When they were safely hidden in the closet, the boy turned to Hans and Gretchen. "I'm Miklös," he said, "Miklös Toth. I was named for the Hungarian regent, Admiral Miklös Horthy."

He laughed. "I guess that was before Papa found out how much Admiral Horthy hates Jews."

"I'm Hans, and this is my sister, Gretchen."

"Thanks for helping me, Hans," Miklös said gravely. "That was a brave thing to do."

Hans was astonished. "Brave?" he echoed. "What I did was nothing! What about what you did? What made you decide to try such a dangerous stunt?"

Miklös shrugged. "They're my people," he said simply, "and they're being sentenced to death, even though they're innocent. Someone had to do something." He leaned forward and began to unlace his boot. "Did any of them make it?"

Hans nodded. "Only about a dozen, I guess. The Nazis shot some of the others."

Miklös sighed. "A dozen. Then it was worth it."

"But you got shot!" Gretchen exclaimed.

"Yes, but I'll live," he told her. "Those on the train will not. It was worth it." He was quiet and thoughtful for a while. "At least we saved a few." Again there was silence.

Gretchen leaned forward. "You said that those were your people," she said softly. "Are you a Jew?"

Miklös nodded. "Yes! And proud of it."

"Then where is your yellow star?" Gretchen asked.

Miklös reached up and whipped off his hat. Hans and Gretchen saw a thick shock of light brown hair framing his thin face. His dark eyes burned. “The order to wear the yellow star came from Karl Adolf Eichmann,” he growled through clenched teeth, glancing down to the breast of his coat where the star should have been, “and I don’t take orders from Eichmann! He and his *Einsatzkommando* are the ones killing my people!”

“But the penalty for not wearing the star is death,” Hans pointed out.

“Eichmann told the Jewish Council that he wants us to wear the star for our protection,” Miklös retorted. “But the real reason is so that he can identify us and kill us. I won’t make it easy for him! Eichmann has killed over four hundred thousand Jews from Hungary. But Admiral Horthy finally ordered a halt to the deportations. There are still four hundred fifty thousand Jews living in Budapest. Eichmann wants us, too.”

Hans frowned. “So why are the trains running again,” he asked, “if Admiral Horthy stopped the deportations?”

“Horthy is old and weak,” Miklös replied. “He’s been the regent of Hungary since 1919. That’s twenty-five years. He’s over seventy now. Besides, the only reason he ordered a halt to the deportations was because the Allies were putting pressure on him. Two days ago, the Arrow Cross—the Hungarian Nazi party—kidnapped Horthy’s son as he was leaving the Royal Palace. They forced Horthy to sign papers turning the government over to the Arrow Cross and naming Szalasi as prime minister. Once the Arrow Cross seized power, the deportations started again. That’s why the train was running today.”

He suddenly held up a hand. “Quiet,” he whispered. “Listen.”

The three listened intently. Gretchen held her breath. Hans crept to the window and peered cautiously out for any signs of movement. A cold fear hung in the stale air of the little closet.

Miklös finally leaned forward and slid his bloody boot from his foot. "I thought I heard somebody, but I guess not," he whispered softly. "We had better stay put for a while, just to be safe." He removed his sock and examined the wound, gently squeezing his foot as he did.

Miklös took off his jacket and ripped a section out of the lining. He tore it into strips and bandaged his foot. "There," he whispered with a satisfied grin, "that will at least slow the bleeding."

He replaced his jacket. "Tell me about yourselves. Where are you from? I've noticed that your German is far better than your Magyar."

Hans laughed. "We're originally from Austria," he said, "but we came through France. Papa has a friend in Budapest who gave him a job in his appliance repair shop. We've been here a little over a year and a half. That's why we're not too fluent in Magyar."

"How old are you, Hans?"

"Fourteen," Hans replied. "And Gretchen is eleven."

"I'll be twelve in January," Gretchen reminded Hans. "How old are you, Miklös?"

"Fourteen," the Jewish boy replied. "I'll be fifteen in January, if I live that long."

Hans felt an urge to witness to Miklös, but he did his best to ignore it, telling himself that he really didn't know the Hungarian boy well enough.

"Papa was a banker," Miklös said abruptly, with a faraway look in his eye. "He was one of the wealthiest in Budapest. But as you know, Jews are no longer allowed to own businesses, so Papa lost the bank." He sighed. "So now we're one of the poorest families in Budapest. We live in two rooms in the basement of one of the Christians' houses." A sudden change came over him as he squared his shoulders and he held his head up proudly. "But my grandpapa is on the Jewish Council," he declared.

The three young people continued to talk in hushed tones for the next half-hour, discussing the war, the Nazi occupation of Hungary, the Jewish situation, and the possibilities of liberation by the Russian army. "The Nazis will lose this war," Miklös declared. "They're losing on all the fronts. I just hope the Russians get here before Eichmann has time to kill all of my people."

Miklös leaned over and studied the bloody bandage around his foot. "Let's see if we can get out of here without being seen," he said. "There's a bicycle hidden on the other side of the foundry. If you can help me get to it, I can coast home on it and push myself along with my good foot."

"You were very fortunate," the wiry-haired doctor said as he finished wrapping Miklös's foot. "If you had to take a Nazi bullet, you couldn't have chosen a better spot. The slug passed through your foot without hitting any bones or damaging any tendons. It should heal quite nicely. But you must stay off it for at least two weeks."

"Two weeks!" Miklös protested. "But I have to . . . I have to be on it. Tomorrow!" He glanced at Hans and Gretchen. "There's something I have to do. I have to!"

The doctor sternly shook his head. "Two weeks," he said emphatically. "If you try to get around on it before then, you run a high risk of getting an infection and may have permanent damage."

He addressed Miklös's father as he dropped his scissors into his black bag and zipped it closed. "See that he follows my orders. This is a clean wound, and the boy was fortunate. But it is very important that he not walk on it."

Herr Toth nodded in agreement. "He'll follow your orders."

"Two weeks," Miklös protested as the physician left. "But I can't sit around for two weeks. I have to—" He paused and looked up at Hans. "Can you and Gretchen help me do something? It's important."

Hans shrugged. "*Ja,* if we can."

Miklös leaned forward and lowered his voice. "Take my camera to the Jozsefvarosi station tomorrow and take pictures of the deportations."

Hans frowned. "What for?"

"I plan to smuggle the pictures out to the Allies," the Hungarian youth replied. "The pictures will prove to the world once and for all what the Third Reich is doing to my people. Maybe it's not too late to stop Eichmann and his *Einsatzkommando* before he destroys the Jews from the face of the earth."

Hans nodded thoughtfully. "*Ja,* we'll do it." He turned to his sister. "Won't we, Gretchen?"

Gretchen nodded slowly.

Miklös grinned. "*Gut!* See, I know a little German, *ja?*" He suddenly grew solemn. "I guess I don't need to tell either of you that it will be dangerous to go back. Extremely dangerous. And if they catch you with my camera, they won't even ask any questions; they'll kill you on the spot. Are you sure you're willing to risk it?"

Hans took a deep breath. "We'll do it."

CHAPTER THREE

JOZSEFVAROSI STATION

A huge red sun was just beginning to peek over the eastern horizon of Budapest. The sky was clear, but a northern wind was blowing dust and bits of trash about the streets, and the weather was unseasonably cold. Gretchen shivered and pulled her coat tighter about her as she and Hans knelt in the bushes behind the Jozsefvarosi freight station.

"That building must be the bookbindery," Hans whispered, pointing to an old brick structure beside the depot. "Can you see the broken window on the north side that Miklös told us about? We can get inside from there. He wants us to take the pictures from the second floor."

Gripping Miklös's heavy camera against his side, Hans covered it with his coat and slipped into the alley. Gretchen followed. Moments later, Hans reached through a broken pane to unlatch the window from the inside. "Careful," he whispered, as he boosted Gretchen up to crawl through. "Watch your step."

"What if someone comes?" Gretchen whispered fearfully when Hans had joined her. "What will they do to us?"

"Miklös says that no one gets here until seven-thirty," Hans answered. He glanced at his watch. "It's just six-fifteen now."

The young people found the second story workroom overlooking the freight station. They crept to the window and peered out. A train of cattle cars was just easing up to the depot. "Miklös was right," Hans said softly. He lifted the camera from beneath his coat and began to focus the lens.

"Hans, look," Gretchen said, pointing.

Hans leaned forward. Two large, black cars pulled up at the freight depot and stopped at the far end. As Hans and Gretchen watched, a number of black-uniformed SS men got out. Several marched to the freight platform and began sliding open the doors of the cars. Three of the men climbed to the top of the cattle cars and took positions on the roof. Hans let out his breath slowly.

Just then, around the corner of the building, a long line of condemned Jews appeared. Rich and poor, young and old, they all shared the same hunted, desperate look. Some clutched battered suitcases or pillowcases containing personal possessions; but each wore a canary yellow, six-pointed Star of David over the left breast. Defeated and doomed, they were being driven by strong, young SS soldiers with automatic weapons and Doberman pinschers on short leashes. A band of green-shirted youths with automatic rifles seemed especially eager for opportunities to bully the poor Jewish people. Within moments the loading platform was swarming with shouting soldiers, snarling dogs, cowering Jews, and crying, frightened children.

Gretchen watched the scene with tears brimming in her eyes. "Look at them, Hans," she sobbed. "Little children who are too young to start school. Old grandmothers who used to bake cookies for their grandchildren, and grandfathers who carved toy whistles. Young men and women who had dreams of getting married and having a family. Mothers with little—" she choked back a sob, "little babies. And they're all going to die, just because they're Jews."

Gretchen ducked her head beneath the windowsill. "I can't—oh, Hans, I can't watch anymore."

Hans wiped the tears from his own eyes and began to snap pictures of the heartbreaking scene below. He bit his lip to keep from crying. "Maybe Miklös is right," he said hoarsely, "maybe our pictures will be a way to stop the killing."

As Hans snapped picture after picture, he winced again and again as he witnessed one act of cruelty after another. His heart went out to the hopeless, persecuted people being loaded onto the train that would take them to their deaths. *Dear God, help us,* he cried silently. *Help us find a way to save these poor people!*

Hans lowered the camera and clenched his teeth in helpless rage. A young woman had fallen at the edge of the platform. A youth in a green shirt stepped over and beat her mercilessly with his rifle until she managed to crawl into the cattle car and collapse on the floor.

"Why, dear God?" Hans wept.

As they had done the day before, the Nazis were cramming each cattle car until it could not possibly hold any more, then placing a single loaf of bread and bucket of water inside before locking the door. By the time the train was half-loaded, Hans had finished a complete roll of film. His heart ached as he slipped to a dark corner of the room to load a second roll.

"Hans!" Gretchen suddenly called. "Come here! Look at this!"

Hans glanced up from the camera. "I can't, Gretchen," he snapped at her, unconsciously venting the anger he felt toward the Nazis. "I'm loading the camera."

"Come here, Hans," Gretchen repeated. "Look at this man."

There was a note of urgency in her voice, and Hans responded. He set Miklös's camera carefully on the floor and rushed back to the window.

The first thing he noticed was a shiny blue Studebaker with blue and yellow flags on each side of the hood. The car was parked beside the cars belonging to the Nazi officers. Behind the cars stood several large trucks, each marked with the insignia of the Red Cross.

"Look at that man, Hans!" Gretchen exclaimed again. "Who is he?"

A man in a long raincoat and broad-brimmed hat stood in the center of the crowded loading platform with a huge black ledger book under his arm. He was shouting at the SS officers. And to Hans's amazement, each time the man took a step forward, the Nazi officers took a step back. *They're afraid of him,* Hans thought. *I wonder who he is?*

"Quick," he told Gretchen, "see if we can get a window open. I want to hear what that man is saying."

With trembling fingers Hans managed to unlatch the window and push it open. A cacophony of sounds from the scene below now floated into the room. "I tell you again. You cannot take these people!" the man with the ledger was shouting. "Many of them are under the protection of the Swedish government. They have protective passports. You are breaking international law, and I will hold you responsible."

Hans frowned. "That man is going to get himself killed," he whispered. "You don't talk to SS officers that way."

The man in the raincoat stooped over, picked up a megaphone, and then raised it to his mouth. "If you have a protective passport, you are under the protection of the royal Swedish government," he bellowed across the crowd. "These people cannot take you. Please raise your hand if you are holding a valid Swedish passport."

Hans and Gretchen held their breath as they watched the drama unfold on the platform below. Perhaps some of these people would go free. But to their disappointment, not a single Jew raised a hand.

"Those of you with protective passports, please raise your hands," the man called through the megaphone again. But as before, no hands were raised.

It's no use, Hans thought sadly. *And this poor man who is trying to help is just going to get himself killed.* Hans glanced sadly at Gretchen and shook his head.

But the man on the platform didn't give up. He opened his huge ledger book and shouted, "I have protective passports for the following people. Please respond when your name is called. Mandl. Friedman. Schwartz. Stern. Veres. Weiss. Wohl." As the man continued to call out names, Hans realized that he was simply calling the most common Jewish surnames. And still, no hands were raised.

It's no use! Hans thought despairingly. *The Nazis will see through this ruse. They'll kill you.* His heart went out to the brave man who was trying so desperately to save these Jews from death, but he knew that the situation was hopeless. The Nazis weren't about to let their prisoners go free just because they claimed to have a "protective passport." At any rate, the Jewish people were too afraid to raise their hands.

Hans noticed several men slipping quietly through the crowd. They whispered something in the ear of each Jewish person as they passed. And to Hans's amazement, hands began to go up.

"That's better," the man with the megaphone and the ledger shouted. "Now, if you have a passport, form a line right over here. My staff will check your passport in just a moment."

Several dozen Jews hurried over to form a ragged line along the edge of the platform. The men who had passed the whispered message through the crowd now hurried over and began to fill out a form for each person. Moving quickly, they asked several questions of each person and penned in information on the document as the Jewish person answered. The men worked at a frantic pace.

Hans turned to Gretchen, who stood at the window with her mouth open. "Gretchen, get down," he whispered. "They'll see you." Gretchen glanced at Hans and obediently dropped to her knees.

"This isn't going to work," Hans told her. "I don't think these people really have passports, and these men are filling them out for them right here. The Nazis aren't going to fall for this. That man is just going to get himself and his staff killed right here on the platform."

"Maybe not, Hans. Look!" said Gretchen excitedly.

The man opened his ledger again and was writing down the name of each Jew as he or she filed past him and showed the new passport. These Jews immediately marched to the waiting trucks and climbed aboard. It was a miracle! The Arrow Cross soldiers and SS officers stood silently watching the entire episode. By now, the line of Jews waiting for passports was several hundred people long.

Hans held his breath as he expected to see the SS officers give the signal to kill these brave men and the Jews they were trying to save. The trucks were nearly full, and yet the line of "passport holders" was still growing.

"Dear God, help this brave but ignorant man," Hans pled softly.

At that moment, a senior SS officer stepped forward and raised his hand. "Enough!" he shouted. "Enough of this!"

Hans winced. *This is it*, he thought. *These people are doomed; the Nazis will massacre them all right here. The camera! This will be horrible, but I need to get it on film for the Allies*. But Hans found that he couldn't move from the window to retrieve the camera. His feet refused to respond.

The Nazi officer turned on the man with the ledger. "No more!" he screamed. "Take the people you have but no more!"

The man with the ledger was already walking quickly toward the waiting Studebaker with the blue and yellow flags, and the Red Cross trucks were rolling from the depot. Hans turned back to Gretchen as the Nazis resumed loading the train. "That was unbelievable!" he exclaimed. "I think that man just saved the lives of nearly three hundred people!"

Hans looked at his watch. "It's seven-fifteen," he gasped. "Let's get out of here!" He dashed over to the corner, snatched up the camera, and hurriedly finished loading it. Tucking it underneath his coat, he and Gretchen hurried from the room.

Moments later, they raced down the hallway on the first floor. "We'll go out the back door," Hans announced. "It'll be faster and safer than using the window."

He paused beneath the open window and handed the camera to Gretchen. "Hold this while I latch the window," he instructed.

Gretchen's gaze darted to the door, and her eyes widened in panic. "Hans."

Hans spun around. The frosted glass panel in the door showed the silhouette of a large figure standing just outside the door. A key was turning in the lock.

CHAPTER FOUR
RAOUL WALLENBERG

The door swung open before Hans and Gretchen could make a move, and they found themselves face to face with a tall man with a huge mustache. The man's mouth fell open in surprise when he saw the intruders, but then he recovered quickly. His lunch pail clattered to the floor. He leaped forward and seized Hans by the wrist. "What are you doing here?" he demanded angrily.

Hans tried to speak, but no words came out. The big man shook him roughly. "What are you doing in here?" he demanded again. "How did you get in here?"

Hans finally found his voice. "There's a broken window. We opened the latch," he croaked.

The man leaned closer. "Why did you come here?" He shook Hans again.

"W-We j-just . . ." Hans stammered. "We j-just came . . ."

His captor suddenly spotted the camera and seized it with his free hand, jerking it from Gretchen's grasp. "Ah-ha! And what is this for?"

Hans's heart sank. *The camera belongs to Miklös! What if this man keeps it? And what if we lose our valuable pictures?*

"We weren't doing anything wrong," Gretchen spoke up. "We just came to take pictures."

"Pictures of what?" The man spun around to face Gretchen, dragging Hans around in the same motion.

Hans stared at Gretchen, pleading silently with his eyes for her not to say any more. But Gretchen didn't notice. "We just wanted pictures of the train and of the way the Nazis are treating the Jews," Gretchen replied. "We took pictures from the upstairs window that overlooks the loading platform at the depot."

The man jerked Hans around to face him again. "Is that true?"

Hans nodded fearfully.

"What do you want with the pictures?"

Hans hesitated, praying desperately. *Lord, how much should I tell this man? Miklös needs these pictures.*

"What are you going to do with the pictures?" the man demanded again.

"A friend of ours wants to send them to the Allies," Hans finally answered, "so they have evidence of what's happening to the Jews here in Budapest. We're hoping the Allies will find a way to stop the killings."

The man seemed stunned by Hans's reply. He shook his head slowly and relaxed his grip on Hans's wrist, almost as if he were unaware that he was doing so. "You're brave kids," he said softly. A faraway look appeared in his eyes, and he stood silently for a moment or two.

Suddenly he thrust the camera at Hans. "Here. You two get out of here before you get into trouble, or before you get me in trouble." He opened the door for them. "I'll keep quiet about this little visit, and I would suggest that you do the same. But, please, don't try this again. It's much too dangerous."

The big man closed the door behind Hans and Gretchen. Hans tucked the camera under his jacket, and he and Gretchen hurried down the alley behind the freight depot.

Hans and Gretchen found Miklös in the little basement room with his foot up on a pillow. Words spilled out as they recounted what had happened.

"So anyway, the trucks rolled out of the station loaded with all those Jewish people," Hans said as he finished the story for Miklös, "and the man just got in his Studebaker and drove away! He must have saved three hundred people. And the Nazis and Arrow Cross just let him leave. It was incredible."

"Wallenberg," Miklös said softly.

Hans frowned. "Who? Do you know this man?"

"Raoul Wallenberg," Miklös repeated. "He's from Sweden, but he came to Budapest to try to save Jews. He's the second secretary of the Royal Swedish Legation."

"The Swedish Legation?" Hans echoed. "Is that like an embassy?"

Miklös nodded. "Sort of. It's where the Swedish minister, Ivan Danielsson, has his offices."

"So is Herr Wallenberg an ambassador?" Gretchen asked.

Miklös shook his head. "He's a diplomat, but a very low ranking one. He doesn't have nearly as much power or influence as an ambassador."

"So why did the Nazis let him do what he did this morning?" Hans asked. "He just had a few men with him, and they didn't have guns or anything—at least, not that I could see. The Nazis and Arrow Cross all had automatic weapons, and I really thought they would kill him. But instead, they let him take all those Jews. Why?"

Miklös shook his head. "Papa says it's a miracle. Wallenberg is a low ranking diplomat, but it's almost as if the Nazis are afraid of him. Papa says that Wallenberg is constantly sending letters and memos to the Nazis, to the Hungarian government, and to the Arrow Cross, warning them that he and his staff are keeping records of the way they treat the Jews. The Allies keep saying that there is going to be a war crimes tribunal when the war is over, and Wallenberg says that he intends to make the Nazis answer for what they do in Budapest."

Hans frowned. "And the Nazis listen to him because of that? Why don't they just kill him?"

The Hungarian boy shrugged. "Maybe they're afraid to."

"He was giving some special kind of papers to the Jews," Gretchen remarked. "He said it was some kind of special passport."

Miklös laughed and reached inside his jacket. "Like this?" He pulled out a piece of paper and unfolded it. Hans and Gretchen saw an official looking blue and yellow document with three gold crowns embossed in the center. The paper was stamped with the Swedish seal and had Ivan Danielsson's signature at the bottom. Miklös's picture was in the upper left corner.

Hans stared at it. "Where did you get that?"

Miklös chuckled. "It's called a *Schützpasse*, or a protective passport. Papa and I got them from the Swedish Legation. Wallenberg told us to never go anywhere without them." Miklös sighed. "Papa's pass once saved his life."

Hans stared at Miklös. "Have you met Wallenberg? Personally?"

Miklös nodded and smiled. "Many times. I often serve as a courier for the legation."

"Taking messages and stuff? Isn't that dangerous?" The questions came from Gretchen.

The Jewish youth shrugged. "Dangerous? Sure! But Wallenberg and the Swedish Legation are working to save my people, and I'll do anything I can to serve them." He fingered the roll of film that Hans had handed him, and his eyes lit up as an idea suddenly occurred to him. "Hey. We just need to get this to the Swedish Legation. Wallenberg can send it out in the diplomatic mail pouch."

Miklös studied the film thoughtfully and then looked at Hans. "Would you do me a big favor? It might be dangerous."

Hans shrugged. "Budapest and danger seem to go together," he replied. "What do you want us to do?"

"Take the film to the Swedish Legation and give it to Wallenberg," Miklös said. "Tell him what's on the film and that I think he can use the pictures as evidence of the Nazi atrocities against the Jewish people. He'll know the best way to use it."

"How do we find the Swedish Legation?" Gretchen asked.

"The legation is on the Buda side of the Danube River," Miklös replied. "It's a big, stone building halfway up St. Gellert's hill on Minerva Street. But don't cross the river at the Ferenc-Jozsef Bridge. You're likely to run into an Arrow Cross checkpoint. Instead, take Rakoczi Avenue to the Erzsebert Bridge and cross there. It's farther that way, but it's safer. Once you cross the bridge, take the first left, and you'll find yourself heading up St. Gellert's hill. Take a right on Minerva Street, and you'll see the legation. It's easy."

Hans smiled. "You seem to know this entire city like your own backyard."

Miklös grinned. "I was born here. Ever since I was little I've been running errands for Papa's bank." He laughed. "Wait till I get back on my feet and have the chance to show you the lower city."

Hans frowned. "The lower city?"

"There's a whole system of tunnels, storm drains, and cisterns beneath the city streets," Miklös explained. "A lot of them were built by the Turks. My cousins and I used to spend hours exploring underground. I can take you from one side of Budapest to the other underground, and the only time we have to come up is to cross the Danube. I'll show you sometime. It's incredible."

He handed the film to Hans. "Just tell Madame Wohl at the front desk of the legation that I sent you and that you need to see Wallenberg. She'll let you in."

Hans pocketed the roll of film. "Take care of that foot, Miklös," he said. "Gretchen and I will take the film to Wallenberg right now. We'll check in tomorrow and see how you're doing."

Miklös carefully lifted his injured foot and crossed his legs. "Thank you, Hans. But be careful. The *Nyalis*—Arrow Cross squads—are everywhere, and they're vicious. If you run into any of them, don't mention Wallenberg, and don't let them know you have the film. They'll kill you on the spot if they know what you are doing."

Hans nodded soberly. "We'll be careful."

Gretchen followed Hans up the stairs, and they passed into the street.

As they stepped around a bomb crater on Pozsonyi Road, Gretchen pointed to a large poster nailed to a telephone pole. "There's another Arrow Cross poster," she whispered.

"DEATH TO THE JEWS!" the poster proclaimed in bold letters. The text underneath insisted that the Jewish people were guilty of signaling Allied bombers with bed sheets, of slaughtering Hungarian children for sacrifices, and of poisoning the city's wells and water supply. "The very presence of these barbaric Jews jeopardizes the safety of every citizen of Budapest," the poster contended. "When all of Hungary is *Judenfrei,* peace and prosperity will return to our land, and we can once again resume our normal lives."

"How can they say that?" Gretchen said hotly. "The Jews haven't done any of those things! It's all a lie!"

"It's just Nazi propaganda," Hans sighed. "No Jew has been found flapping a bed sheet from a rooftop, or killing a child, or poisoning the water. But if the Nazis can spread their hatred of Jews to the Hungarian people, their own crimes and cruelties will seem justified." He pointed to the wall of a clothing shop. "There's another one asking citizens to report anyone suspected of helping Jews obtain papers illegally."

Hans glanced up the street. "That's Rakoczi Street at the corner. We're almost to the river." He and Gretchen crossed the street to avoid a pile of debris from a bombed building.

Gretchen grabbed his arm. "Hans, look. Arrow Cross! Let's go back before they see us."

It was too late. Three teenage boys and a girl, all dressed in green shirts and carrying automatic rifles, had stepped from the doorway of a house less than a hundred meters up the street. When they saw Hans and Gretchen, the *Nyalis* hurried in their direction.

"Hey you!" one of the boys called. "Come here! We want to talk to you."

"Stay calm," Hans whispered softly, "and trust the Lord. He'll see us through this."

"Well, look at this cute little blond," one of the Arrow Cross youths sneered, reaching out a dirty hand to stroke one of Gretchen's braids. "I could go for a doll like you, sweetheart." He laughed, watching closely for Hans's reaction.

Hans resisted an impulse to slug the boy.

"So where are you two going?" the Arrow Cross girl asked Hans as she stepped forward and pointed her rifle at his throat. "You don't seem too happy to see us."

"Just heading across the river," Hans replied, praying silently for the right words to say.

"Across the river, huh?" the girl responded. "That doesn't tell us much, does it? Now, I'm going to ask you again; where are you going?" She increased the pressure against Hans's neck.

"Just heading across the river," Hans said again, "to see a friend."

One of the Arrow Cross boys stepped forward. "A friend, huh?" he said. "Who?"

Hans thought back to the warning Miklös had given. "Don't mention Wallenberg," he had said.

Hans drew a deep breath. "Just a friend," he answered again.

"He's not telling us much, is he?" the girl with the rifle said sharply.

"No, he's not," the first tough replied, "but I have an idea. We're just a block or two from the river. Let's shoot this rooster and toss him in. The girl can come with us."

"No!" Gretchen screamed. "You can't! You just can't. Please. You can't."

The Arrow Cross girl laughed as she lowered the rifle and slapped Gretchen across the face. "I say we shoot them both," she declared. "This girl dies first."

CHAPTER FIVE
THE ARROW CROSS

Hans stared at the four Arrow Cross youths. He reached out and drew Gretchen close to him, as if he could somehow protect her from harm. *Lord, help us!* he prayed desperately.

"You can't do this," Gretchen insisted again. "We haven't done anything to hurt you." She began to sob.

One of the boys stepped forward and jerked Gretchen from Hans's grasp. "March!" he ordered, dragging her along by one braid.

"You too, love," the Arrow Cross girl said, prodding Hans in the back with her rifle. "We want to see how well you swim."

Fear swept over Hans as the four Arrow Cross toughs marched him and Gretchen toward the river. *Father, help us,* he prayed silently in desperation. *There's nothing we can do. There are four of them, and they all have guns. And I know they won't think twice about shooting us and throwing our bodies in the river.*

He noticed that their captors turned and followed the Corso, the wide boulevard along the Pest side of the Danube, toward the Ferenc-Jozsef Bridge. Miklös had warned them about trying to cross that very bridge, and now it looked as if that would be the same spot in which he and Gretchen would die. If that particular bridge was an Arrow Cross checkpoint, the youths that held them captive would be more likely to carry through on their threat to kill them, if only to prove themselves to their comrades.

An Arrow Cross officer and two skinny youths with automatic weapons were guarding the approach to the bridge. "Don't let them kill us," Gretchen begged, dropping to her knees at the officer's feet. "Please, don't let them kill us!"

A look of annoyance crossed the man's face. "Get her out of here," he snarled to the four *Nyalis*. Turning his back on Gretchen, he stepped forward to challenge an automobile that was slowly approaching the bridge. The car braked to a stop, and the driver rolled down his window.

Hans stared at the vehicle. It was the blue Studebaker from the freight station. Wallenberg's car! A blue and yellow Swedish flag on each side of the hood confirmed his identification, and a bold idea leaped into his mind.

Hans peered into the car. But the young man at the wheel obviously was not Wallenberg, and the rest of the car was empty. His confidence wavered.

"Let's go!" the Arrow Cross girl ordered, shoving Hans toward the bridge. It was now or never. Hans spun around and slammed the girl against the iron railing of the bridge, causing her to lose her balance and drop her weapon to the pavement. He dodged around the two *Nyalis* behind him and leaped for the driver's side of the Studebaker, slamming his body against the door with an impact that startled the driver.

"Help us, please," Hans begged. The words came in a rush. "Miklös Toth sent us! We have to see Wallenberg! We have film that he must see."

The Arrow Cross girl had recovered her rifle. Now she advanced slowly toward the automobile with her weapon trained on Hans. Rage glittered in her eyes. "Now," she snarled savagely, "you die! Right here." She threw the rifle to her shoulder.

The driver of the Studebaker leaped from the car to stand in front of Hans. "Wait!" he shouted, holding up one hand. "You can't shoot an unarmed citizen here on the street."

"Get out of my way," the Arrow Cross girl growled. "You can't stop me."

Hans fumbled in his pocket for the film. "Here," he said, thrusting the roll into the driver's hands. "Take it to Wallenberg!"

The man twisted around and thrust Hans into the open door of the Studebaker. "Get in," he urged in a whisper. He spun around to face the Arrow Cross squad. "I'm Vilmos Langfelder from the Royal Swedish Legation, and I speak for Wallenberg and Minister Danielsson. These two young people are under the protection of the Swedish government, and I forbid you to harm them in any way."

The Arrow Cross girl stalked toward the car. "You can't stop me," she challenged.

Langfelder boldly seized the barrel of her rifle and shoved the muzzle toward the sky. The girl wrestled with him for possession of the weapon, but he snatched it from her grasp and thrust it at the Arrow Cross officer standing nearby. "Sir, call off these troops. If they harm these two young people, they are breaking international law, and the royal legation will hold you responsible. Now, call off these troopers!"

The officer barked an order in Magyar, and the girl stepped back sullenly.

Langfelder quickly advanced toward the youth that had a grip on Gretchen's coat. "Release her," he ordered, and the boy complied. Langfelder hurried Gretchen to the car. "Get in," he urged.

As Gretchen scrambled into the front seat, Langfelder leaped in beside her, jerking the automobile into gear and stepping on the accelerator. The Arrow Cross squad hurried to one side to allow them to cross the bridge.

"Danke schön," Hans breathed as the Studebaker accelerated up the slope at the far side of the bridge. "That took courage! They meant business. I'm amazed that you could back them down that way."

The driver grinned. "I learned that from Wallenberg," he replied. He let out his breath in a long sigh of relief. "To be honest with you, I guess I even surprised myself."

He guided the car through a gentle curve, then slowed for a turn into a narrow alley. "I'm Wallenberg's driver, Vilmos Langfelder," he said. "It's fortunate I came along when I did, or you two would be swimming in the Danube."

Hans nodded soberly. "It was beginning to look that way." He took a deep breath. "I'm Hans Von Edler, and this is my sister, Gretchen."

"Glad to meet you," the man responded. "Did you say you know Miklös Toth?"

"Miklös had us take pictures of the Nazis loading the Jewish people onto the trains," Hans replied. "He wants us to give the film to Wallenberg so that he can present the pictures to the Allies as evidence against the Nazis."

Langfelder nodded. "Miklös is one clever boy," he replied. "If all the Jews were as determined as he is, the Nazis wouldn't stand a chance." The car swung into a narrow driveway and slowed to a stop behind a handsome stone building proudly flying the blue and yellow flag of Sweden. "Well, here we are," Langfelder said as he opened the car door. "Wallenberg will soon have your film."

He led Hans and Gretchen around the corner of the building. Hans saw a huge crowd of desperate people jostling each other for places in line in front of the legation. Hans knew instinctively that they were Jews. Langfelder stopped and let out a sigh. "These poor people," he breathed. "Wallenberg is their only hope. Unless they can get their hands on one of his passes, they are doomed to execution, and they know it. The Jews are only allowed outdoors from two until five each afternoon, but many of these people have taken a desperate chance and have been here ever since daybreak." He shook his head. "I hope we can save some of them."

Langfelder hurried back toward the alley. "We'll have to go in the back way," he told Hans. "We'll never make it through that throng." Unlocking a back door, he ushered Hans and Gretchen inside.

"Wait here," he told them. "Since you're a friend of Miklös Toth, I want you to meet Wallenberg if he has time. I'll be right back." His footsteps echoed on the blue tile floor as he hurried away.

The room they were in was attractively painted a beautiful blue and gold. A large picture of some snowy mountains hung in a gilded frame on the wall. A flag of Sweden hung on another wall.

Langfelder returned moments later, accompanied by a thin man of medium height with dark eyes and thinning hair. The man looked tired, but he had a friendly smile. His eyes burned with an intensity that reminded Hans of Miklös.

"Vilmos tells me that you are friends of Miklös Toth," the man said as he shook Hans's hand. He bowed to Gretchen. "Miklös is one of our most trustworthy couriers, and we are honored by your visit." He raised one hand to his mouth to cover a cough. "I'm Raoul Wallenberg, second secretary of the Royal Swedish Legation."

Wallenberg winked at Gretchen. “That sounds like an impressive title, don’t you think?” He grinned. “Actually, I am not of a high diplomatic rank, but don’t tell that to Eichmann. I want him to think I’m important so he’ll listen to what I have to say about the Jews.”

Wallenberg opened his left hand, and Hans and Gretchen saw that he held the precious roll of film. “So Miklös thought I should have this, did he? What’s on it?”

“Pictures, Herr Wallenberg,” Hans answered politely. “We took photographs of the Nazis loading the Jews on the train at the Jozsefvarosi station this morning. Miklös said that you could use the photos as evidence of Nazi atrocities against the Jews.”

The man’s eyes widened. “Excellent idea!” He thought for a moment and then glanced at Vilmos Langfelder. “Miklös may have just given us a valuable weapon. Let’s contact Tom Veres and find out if he’s willing to accept a special mission on behalf of his people.”

Wallenberg turned back to Hans and Gretchen. “We know a young Jewish man who is an excellent photographer. We’ll approach him about taking some additional photos, but please, don’t attempt any more by yourselves. It’s far too risky.”

“We don’t mind taking risks,” Hans replied softly.

The man laughed. “You sound just like Miklös,” he replied. “He’s the bravest fellow I’ve ever met, and he has a real heart for his people.”

“We just met him yesterday,” Hans replied. He quickly told the diplomat the story of Miklös’s attempted rescue of the Jews on the death train. Wallenberg shook his head when he was through.

“Isn’t that boy something?” he exclaimed. “I don’t think I’ve ever known a young man with more character or more courage than Miklös Toth.” A look of concern crossed his features. “How badly was he hurt?”

"The doctor said that Miklös has to stay off his feet for two weeks," Hans answered, "but that he should recover with no permanent damage."

"Thank God for that," Wallenberg said.

He glanced at his driver. "Who'll take his place for the next two weeks? Miklös is our most dependable courier."

Hans hesitated, then spoke up. "What does a courier do? Maybe Gretchen and I could help."

"It's becoming riskier as the Arrow Cross squads become more vicious," Wallenberg replied, "but many times a young person can go where an adult would not get through. We use young people to deliver passes and food and to warn prominent Jews when we learn that the Arrow Cross or the Nazis are planning action against them. Miklös is one of the best. He knows this city better than anyone we've met."

"We don't know Budapest as well as Miklös does," Hans said, "but we'll be glad to help in any way we can."

"You need to check with your parents first," Wallenberg told him.

"Papa will give his permission," Hans assured him. "I know he will."

"Do you have a telephone?"

"*Ja,* there's one in the repair shop where Papa works," Hans said. "The owner is a Jew who has put the business and phone in Papa's name. There won't be a problem there. We live right over the shop."

Wallenberg nodded. "*Gut*." He drew a card from the breast pocket of his coat and scribbled a telephone number on it. "Check with your father and then give us a call. You may be able to help save the lives of some Jews."

A tall man hurried down the hall and approached Wallenberg. "Sir, could we talk?" He eyed Hans and Gretchen warily. "Eichmann just had a long meeting with Gabor Vajna, the Arrow Cross minister of the interior, and you need to be briefed on it. Some crucial decisions were made that will directly affect the Jewish situation."

"This is Lars Berg," Wallenberg said to his young visitors. "He's on staff here at the legation."

He turned back to Lars. "Hans and Gretchen are friends of Miklös Toth, and we can trust them. For the sake of time, why don't you brief me right now? What was discussed in Eichmann's meeting with Vajna?"

"Eichmann wants to send fifty thousand Budapest Jews to the Third Reich immediately," Lars said, "and Vajna agreed to it. Also, they plan to construct a central ghetto in the area of the main synagogue. After the fifty thousand are gone, the remaining Jews are to be herded—for lack of a better term—into the ghetto or the four camps outside Budapest."

Wallenberg shook his head. "That's a bad sign." He sighed. "They're planning a major pogrom against the Jews."

"What's a pogrom?" Gretchen asked.

Wallenberg sighed again. "A massacre, Gretchen. It looks as if *Einsatzkommando* Eichmann is planning to eradicate the rest of the Budapest Jews in one fell swoop."

Lars Berg nodded soberly. "It looks that way." He wrung his hands. "But here's the worst part, sir. After today, our protective passes are not to be honored. Vajna says that they're worthless."

Wallenberg bit his lip, and a frown crossed his face. "If that's true," he said slowly, "the Jews of Budapest don't stand a chance. Eichmann will kill them all, and there's nothing we can do."

CHAPTER SIX
BARONESS KEMENY

"Papa," Gretchen said as they finished their supper in the tiny apartment over the repair shop, "Hans wants to ask you something."

Hans looked up in surprise from his bowl of *Gulyassuppe*. "I do?"

"Ja," Gretchen prodded, "you know . . . about helping Wallenberg?"

"Oh, *ja*." Hans cleared his throat. "Papa, we have something important to ask you, but please listen to the whole thing before you say *ja* or *nein*. *Ja?*"

Papa nodded agreeably as he set his spoon back in his bowl. His eyes twinkled as he looked from Hans to Gretchen. "So what are you two up to now?"

Hans took a deep breath. "Papa, the Nazis and the Arrow Cross *Nyalis* are killing thousands of Jewish people, and somebody ought to do something about it. The Allies are winning the war, but by the time they get to Budapest, it might be too late for the Jews. *Ja?*"

Papa nodded and glanced at Mr. Semestyen, the Jewish shop owner and landlord. "*Ja,* something needs to be done. What do you have in mind?"

"Papa, there's someone who is doing something to help the Jews. His name is Raoul Wallenberg, and he works for the Royal Swedish Legation. He has a whole department with over four hundred people working for him in the legation. They call it Section C. Their main purpose is to save Jewish people."

Mr. Semestyen, a bald-headed little man with a stocky build, nodded and leaned forward. "Wallenberg is a good man. He is doing all he can to save my people from Eichmann and his *Einsatzkommando*." His eyes suddenly welled up with tears. "I just wish Wallenberg had been here in time to save Emma and the girls."

Mr. Semestyen's family had been visiting relatives in the countryside when Eichmann and his troops had first come to Hungary. The *Einsatzkommando* squads had raided the rural areas of Hungary first, and Mr. Semestyen's wife and daughters had been sent to the death camp at Auschwitz, Poland.

Mr. Semestyen wiped the tears away with the back of his hand. "I just wish Wallenberg had come to Hungary sooner."

Gretchen slipped over and hugged the little Jewish man. "We do, too, Herr Semestyen," she said softly.

Mr. Semestyen patted her arm. "*Danke,* Gretchen," he said. "You're a sweet girl."

The little Jewish man leaned back in his chair and began to describe the heroic work of Wallenberg and the Swedish Legation. He told of Wallenberg's idea of issuing the *Schützpasses*, of his bravery in challenging Eichmann and daring to rescue people from the death trains, and of his tireless efforts to help the Jews by starting soup kitchens and hospitals and by providing shelter in the "yellow star" houses. "Right now," he finished, "Raoul Wallenberg and the Swedish Legation seem to be the only barrier of protection between my people and Colonel Eichmann. The other neutral legations have followed Wallenberg's lead and are issuing a few passes of their own, but if Wallenberg and the Swedish Legation decide to abandon us, my people are doomed."

"Papa," Hans said timidly, "Herr Wallenberg and the people at the Swedish Legation want Gretchen and me to help them with their rescue work. They want us to be couriers. You know, run errands and deliver messages and food. Wallenberg says that he needs someone to take Miklös's place."

"Who is Miklös?" Papa asked.

"The boy we told you about yesterday," Gretchen chimed in. "You know, the one who tried to save some Jews from the death train."

Papa nodded. "*Ja,* I remember." He hesitated. "Won't that be awfully dangerous? The Arrow Cross thugs are even assaulting the non-Jews now."

Hans expelled his breath sharply. "*Ja,* Papa, we are aware of the danger. But we'll be careful and try not to take any chances. Gretchen and I decided that it will be worth the risk if we can help save some Jewish people."

Mr. Semestyen slowly nodded his head. "Hans and Gretchen, you're good kids. Maybe there's hope for this old world if there are a few decent people like you and your papa and our friend Mr. Wallenberg. When people like Hitler and Eichmann are in power, the world seems like a mighty dark place. But people like you are a ray of light. Maybe there is hope."

Hans shot a pleading look in his father's direction. "Please, Papa? We want to help."

Papa sighed. "I don't know, Hans," he said slowly. He began to toy with the ends of his mustache, and Hans could see that he was deep in thought. Hans and Gretchen waited patiently.

Mr. Semestyen knelt beside the sofa and pulled an old radio from its hiding place. After plugging it in he began to fiddle with the knobs. Soft music wafted from the radio. Mr. Semestyen made a final adjustment and then sat down with a look of satisfaction on his face. "I know it's illegal, but I'd be lost without my radio," he said.

The music suddenly cut off, and Mr. Semestyen glanced at the radio with a look of irritation.

"Attention! Attention!" a man's voice suddenly blared from the radio. "Please stand by for an important announcement from the foreign minister."

"This is Foreign Minister Kemeny," another man's voice announced. "The following protective passes must be honored: three thousand from the Papal Nuncio, three thousand Swiss, and three thousand Swedish. Anyone holding such a pass must not be harmed. Repeat. These pass holders are not to be harmed!"

Hans sighed deeply with relief at the conclusion of the message. "Then the passes are still good," he rejoiced. "It's my guess that Wallenberg had something to do with this."

Papa cleared his throat. "This man Wallenberg seems to be a real servant to the Jewish people," he observed. "I don't know if he is a Christian or not, but he seems to have a real servant's heart."

He cleared his throat again. "Hans and Gretchen, if there's one thing I would wish for each of you, it's that you would learn to have servants' hearts. When you become a servant, you become more like our Savior, the Lord Jesus. This man Wallenberg is doing everything he can to help the Jewish people, and I'm going to allow you to help him in any way you can. But, be careful! Budapest is a dangerous place to live right now, and I don't want you taking any unnecessary chances. Promise me that you'll be careful."

Hans nodded. "*Ja,* Papa, we will," he promised.

Gretchen hugged her father. "*Danke,* Papa," she whispered. "We'll be careful."

Papa pulled his pocket watch from his waistband and glanced at it. "It's getting late. We'd better head for bed."

"Goodnight, Herr Semestyen," Gretchen called, as the Jewish shopkeeper headed for his room.

"*Guten tag,* Frau," Hans said politely, as Madame Wohl opened the legation door to admit him and Gretchen. "Did you hear the announcement on the radio last night? The *Schützpasses* are to be honored! Baron Kemeny announced it last night!"

Madame Wohl smiled broadly. "I didn't hear the announcement myself," she replied, "but I've heard all about it from every staff member to walk through this door this morning! We're rejoicing at the news."

"What made the Arrow Cross government change its mind?" Gretchen asked. "Vajna had decided not to honor the passes."

"It was Wallenberg's doing," the woman replied. "I sometimes think that man can work miracles. As I understand it, he called Baroness Kemeny—the wife of the minister of the interior—he met her at a diplomatic reception a month or so ago, and they became friends. . . . Anyway, as I was saying, Wallenberg called her and told her about Vajna's decision not to honor our passes. The baroness put pressure on her husband to reverse the decision and honor the passes, and it worked. For right now, at least, the *Schützpasses* are good, and that will save some lives."

"We came to see Herr Wallenberg," Hans informed her, "to tell him that Papa gave us permission to help as couriers for the legation."

Madame Wohl nodded. "*Gut!* He's in his office right now, though he should be home in bed. He's had almost no sleep in the last three days. That man simply doesn't know when to stop! He's about to drop from exhaustion, but anytime the phone rings with another emergency situation, he's right there to help. He has a passion to save our people, and he's not going to rest until we're out of danger."

She turned from the desk and started down the hall. "Come on. I'll take you to him."

The telephone rang just then, and Madame Wohl sighed as she picked up the receiver. "Royal Swedish Legation," she said.

She listened for a moment, then said, "*Ja,* he's here. I'll tell him immediately. *Ja*, I'm sure he'll be right there to see what he can do."

She hung up the receiver. "Another emergency. Let's go tell Herr Wallenberg."

Madame Wohl hurried down the hallway with Hans and Gretchen right on her heels. She burst into Wallenberg's office without even bothering to knock. Wallenberg was at his desk, and he looked up in surprise as they entered.

"The Arrow Cross raided several of the yellow star houses on Jokai Street last night," Madame Wohl blurted. "They marched more than a hundred people to the Danube and shot them."

Wallenberg hung his head in sorrow with a look of utter defeat on his somber face.

"Perhaps we can help the others, sir," Madame Wohl continued. "According to the informant, the Gendarmes and Arrow Cross marched nearly two thousand others to the Bekasmegyer brick-yards. There's a death train scheduled to pick them up this evening."

Wallenberg leaped to his feet. "Call the Swiss consul and the Red Cross," he instructed Madame Wohl. "I want the trucks at Bekasmegyer immediately." He seized his ledger book, a huge stack of blank *Schützpasses*, and his knapsack. "Did we get in touch with Tom Veres? I want pictures!"

The woman shook her head. "*Nein*. We've been unable to get through."

Wallenberg groaned as he eyed the camera on his desk. "We need the pictures. We must begin to record these events as evidence for the Allies."

He seemed to become aware of Hans and Gretchen for the first time. "Did your father approve your working with us?" he asked eagerly.

Hans nodded. "*Ja,* Herr Wallenberg. We can help."

"Gut!" Wallenberg exclaimed. "Then I have an assignment for you. Right now!"

He dropped the knapsack on the floor, picked up the camera, and thrust it into Hans's hands. "I saw your photos from the Jozsefvarosi station, and they were very good. I want you to go with us to Bekasmegyer and shoot some more. It'll be dangerous, but we need your help."

"What about me?" Gretchen demanded.

"You can help, too," Wallenberg replied. He turned to Madame Wohl. "Let Gretchen help you with the filing of the new *Schützpasses*. I dare not take her to Bekasmegyer; it will be extremely dangerous."

He grabbed the knapsack from the floor. "Ready, Hans? Let's find Vilmos Langfelder and get moving. We're about to embark on an adventure that you will never forget."

CHAPTER SEVEN
THE BEKASMEGYER BRICKYARD

Nine-year-old Nina Weiss cringed in fear as the front door shook with blows from a clenched fist. "Time's up!" a rough German voice called. "Open the door and come to the courtyard. Now!"

Nina crept to the front window and, knowing that she was breaking one of the restrictions against Jews, peered out. She sucked in her breath sharply. The street below her fifth-story apartment was filled with Hungarian Gendarmes in brown uniforms, black-booted Nazi soldiers in gray coats, and the green shirts of the dreaded Arrow Cross. Her heart throbbed with fear.

Twenty minutes earlier, SS officers with bullhorns had swept through the compounds of the six-story stone buildings, broadcasting the announcement that all residents were to be in the courtyard in twenty minutes with a coat and one suitcase. And now the twenty minutes were up.

"Come, Nina," her mother called frantically. "We must go." She swept two-year-old Isaac up into her arms and picked up her suitcase. Nina hurried to her side as she opened the door.

The burly soldier outside the door grabbed Nina's mother and flung her against the wall with such force that Isaac banged his head and began to cry. "Drop your suitcase," the soldier ordered, and Nina's mother complied. The Nazi flung the suitcase open and hastily searched for valuables. Finding nothing of value, he snapped it closed and shoved it in Nina's direction. "Carry it," he barked. With a trembling hand, Nina gripped the handle.

As Nina and her mother joined the crowd of defeated Jews who stumbled down the narrow flight of stairs, they stepped around an Arrow Cross woman and an old man. Nina saw the woman snatch the watch from the old man's wrist, then reach for his glasses.

The elderly man drew back. "Please," he pleaded, "I can't see without them."

The Arrow Cross woman seized the glasses and stuffed them into her coat pocket without even folding the ear pieces. "You won't need them where you're going," she snapped. "Now move. *Mach schnell!*"

A Gendarme at the bottom of the stairs marched Nina and her mother across the courtyard and into the street. Nina's mother shifted Isaac from her right arm to her left. She held his head against her shoulder and rocked him back and forth to quiet his crying.

The street was filled with condemned Jews. Some of the captives had been driven out into the bitter cold without even being allowed to take their coats. The columns of marching Jews merged with one another and swelled in size until they filled even the widest boulevards. Nina switched the suitcase to her other hand and pulled her scarf lower over her eyes to shield her face from the wintry October drizzle. She looked about at the other marchers in the street.

Most of them were women: women carrying infants and little children, women sick and pregnant, women without husbands. She noticed that none of the boys in the crowd was older than twelve years, and that there were very few men under seventy. The healthy men and boys had been sent to the forced labor battalions along with her papa and older brother, Jacob; only those too sick or crippled to serve had been spared.

The fugitives stumbled along tree-lined streets, past the stores and shops and synagogues that had once been part of their everyday lives. They marched past neighbors and friends who simply turned and looked the other way as the sea of hopeless humanity swept past.

Nina hurried to catch up with her mother. "Mama," she whispered, "where are they taking us?"

"Don't talk!" was the only answer she received.

Nina winced as shots rang out from time to time. She saw people fallen or wounded; she saw other people stop to help them and get shot, too. The guards simply shot anyone who stumbled and fell or was too tired or weak to continue the march.

By nightfall hundreds of weary Jews finally stopped at a brickyard in the northern suburb of Bekasmegyer. High walls surrounded the yard and the tall drying sheds, making Nina think immediately of a prison. Deep pits marked the ground between the sheds.

The cursing Arrow Cross soldiers and Gendarmes pushed and whipped the Jews into the brickyard, using their rifle butts to punish anyone who hesitated. Some people slipped in the mud and were trampled. Others stumbled in the darkness and fell into the drying pits. The soldiers simply shot them. Nina was overcome with horror.

"Hurry, Nina," her mother urged, speaking for the first time in hours. "Perhaps we can get inside one of the sheds and get out of this rain." Nina ran to catch up. As she entered the darkness of the shed, she suddenly realized that her hands were empty. Where was the suitcase?

The marchers pushed and fought their way inside the shed and gratefully sank to the floor, packing themselves in so tightly that there was no room to lie down or even to move. Nina rested her head against her mother.

"Oh, Mama," she sobbed, "what are they going to do to us? Where are we going?" Her mother didn't answer but simply started stroking Nina's head. Nina heard her crying and felt her body shake with sobs.

The long, long night was filled with groans and cries and wails from the suffering people around her. People called out the names of relatives. Nina was cold and hungry and tired, but the night would bring little relief. There was no bathroom. Nina held out as long as she could but finally gave in to the urgent demand. In her misery she thought of the poor people who had not been fortunate enough to obtain the shelter of the sheds; they now lay outside in the cold rain. Some of them did not even have coats.

"Dear God in heaven," she cried quietly, "please help us! Please help those poor people outside in the cold and the rain!" Exhausted by the long day of terror, she fell asleep.

At midnight there was an air raid, and Nina heard the Allied planes bombing nearby factories. The whine of the planes and the explosions of the bombs kept her awake for nearly an hour.

The morning light brought no relief in the desperate situation of the helpless Jews huddled inside the brickyard. Nina woke to the sound of a rough German voice amplified through a bullhorn. "You will stay where you are until we give further orders," the voice declared. "There will be no escape attempts. If anyone tries, we will machine-gun the entire group!"

Nina shuddered.

Throughout the long day, the guards offered no food or water to the suffering Jews. Many of the prisoners had been injured as they entered the brickyard the night before, but there was no medical attention given. And there were no bathrooms. The stench of human waste filled the darkness of the airless shed.

Late that afternoon Nina heard the rumble of trucks as they rolled into the brickyard. Suddenly, the huge doors at the end of the shed were thrown open, and daylight streamed in. A man in a frayed raincoat and broad-brimmed hat stepped into the doorway with a megaphone in his hand. "*Ich bin* Wallenberg!" he shouted. "I am Wallenberg! We have come to help you! We have food, and there are doctors and nurses with me. If someone near you is sick or injured, please help him or her from the shed so that we may attend to them. I'll take anyone with a protective pass back to Budapest."

Nina looked about, but no one moved. The captive Jews stared up with glazed eyes like wild animals trapped by a light. They had simply given up hope, having been herded like animals and marched for hours.

"Listen to me," Wallenberg called. "You now have food and water and toilets. There are doctors and nurses with me to help those who need it. Please help those around you."

The doctors and nurses moved into the darkness of the shed. Flashlight beams swept across the sea of despairing faces.

And from the far corner of the room, a voice began to chant: "*Shema Yisrael, Adonai Eloheinu, Adonai Ehad*—Hear, O Israel, the Lord is our God, the Lord is One." Within moments, hundreds of voices joined in, until the words of faith seemed to fill the shed. The lifeless Jews had become people again, encouraged by the presence of a man who cared what happened to them.

Nina felt her mother stroking her hair. "Oh, Nina," she sobbed. "It's Wallenberg!"

Within minutes, the brickyard became a scene of noisy confusion as the hopeful Jews poured from the drying sheds. Wallenberg jumped atop a loading platform and issued orders through his megaphone. "All those with Swedish *Schützpasses* form a line over here," he shouted, pointing to one corner of the brickyard. "Those with Swiss passes over there, Red Cross there, Portuguese there, and Vatican there," he continued, pointing to various spots.

The Jews ran chaotically around the brickyard. They changed lines and jostled each other for good places as Wallenberg backed his trucks into position for loading. Nina's mother seized her hand. "Come, Nina," she whispered urgently. "We have no pass, but perhaps we can get onto one of the trucks."

The crowd of frantic women surged toward the trucks. Nina found herself pulled from her mother's grip by the eager, jostling people around her. She slipped and fell.

Someone stepped on her leg, and she cried out in pain. Somehow she managed to scramble to her feet and avoid being trampled by the frantic crowd.

"Mama!" she cried out. Several meters ahead, her mother had reached the refuge of one of the trucks. Nina saw her hand Isaac up to a woman on the back of the truck and then scramble up herself. Nina tried desperately to squeeze through, but the people around her pushed and shoved as frantically as she did. Her heart sank as the truck pulled away without her.

In panic, Nina looked around the brickyard. The other trucks were nearly full, and there was no way she could ever hope to push her way through the crowd to find a place. She would be left behind. Her eyes swam with tears.

There was a large, blue car with blue and yellow flags parked by the front gate. Nina ran toward it. She stumbled and fell, got up, and fell again.

CHAPTER EIGHT

RESCUES

Hans was snapping pictures of the noisy brickyard scene from the safety of the back seat of Wallenberg's Studebaker. He lowered the camera in time to see a young girl dash toward the car. Hans rolled down the window.

"Help me, please," the girl begged as she approached the car. "Mama got on one of the trucks, but I couldn't. And I don't have a *Schützpasse!*" She began to cry.

Hans threw the door open. "Get in, quickly," he urged. The girl scrambled in beside him. "Lie down on the floor so the Arrow Cross won't see you," Hans told her as he slammed the door closed. She immediately complied.

"What's your name?" Hans asked.

"Nina Weiss."

Vilmos Langfelder and Raoul Wallenberg scrambled into the front seats just then, and the car sped from the brickyard. A moment later, Nina rose from her hiding place on the floor. Wallenberg saw her. "What?" he exclaimed in surprise.

Hans leaned forward. "Please don't put her out," he begged. "Her mother is on one of the trucks, but she didn't make it. Please, don't put her out."

Nina's face revealed her fear.

"Put her out?" Wallenberg echoed. "Of course we won't." He grinned suddenly. "Hey, Vilmos, we just rescued one more than we thought."

Wallenberg turned to Nina and asked gently, "What's your name, child?"

"Nina," the girl answered shyly. "Nina Weiss."

"Well, Nina," Wallenberg told her kindly, "you just relax and don't worry about a thing. Everything's going to be all right now. The trucks are taking the people to the safe houses, and we'll find your mother when she gets off."

He turned to Langfelder. "Vilmos, follow the trucks to the Jokai Street houses. You can take me back to the legation after we help Nina find her mother."

Nina began to cry softly. Hans slid closer to her and put an arm around her, and she laid her head on his shoulder.

Wallenberg reached for his knapsack. "Are you hungry, Nina?"

Nina nodded.

November came to Budapest as Hans and Gretchen spent the next several days running errands and delivering food and *Schützpasses* for the legation. Even though they were Austrian, and not Jewish, Wallenberg issued them both *Schützpasses* and insisted that they carry them at all times. The Arrow Cross increased their reign of terror, and both young people were appalled and saddened by the unspeakable acts of cruelty that they witnessed. They soon learned to pause and ask God for personal safety each time they left the apartment to run a "mission."

They made it a point to visit Miklös every other evening to check on his healing progress and to report on their activities. Every Sunday, as he had before the Arrow Cross regime came to power, Papa took them to a worship service. This service was held with a small group of believers in a basement.

The Russian troops had successfully fought their way through the Carpathian mountain passes and were now bearing down on the city of Budapest itself. The Nazis were clearly losing, and it was simply a matter of time before the Russians would drive them from the country. Wallenberg and the Swedish Legation realized that they were in a race against time. Their mission was to keep as many Jews as possible out of the hands of Eichmann and his *Einsatzkommando* until the Russian victory. Wallenberg and his staff made rescues on a daily basis, escorting the grateful Jews they rescued to yellow star houses and providing them with food and medical attention.

"It's *gut* to have you with us again," Hans said as he followed Miklös and Gretchen down the alley behind Jokai Square. "I imagine you're glad to get out."

Miklös laughed. "*Ja,* it's *gut* to be on my feet again," he answered. "That was the longest two weeks of my life."

"How's your foot?" Gretchen asked.

Miklös shrugged. "It doesn't hurt. It just feels, oh . . . kind of weak, I guess."

Hans glanced at his watch. "We had better hurry. Herr Wallenberg wanted us there at nine o'clock this morning, and we're going to have to watch for the Arrow Cross squads."

"Why are we going this way?" Miklös asked. "Have the Arrow Cross set up checkpoints at the Erzsebert Bridge?"

Hans turned in surprise. "I guess we forgot to tell you," he replied. "We're not going to the legation, so we don't have to cross the Danube. Wallenberg has set up his headquarters on Ulloi Avenue so that he can be closer to the Yellow Star houses and the Central Ghetto. It's safer this way—fewer chances of running into Arrow Cross *Nyalis*."

"Speaking of the Arrow Cross, there's a couple right now," Miklös exclaimed. "Quick! Follow me." He ducked into a doorway with Hans and Gretchen behind him.

Miklös peered cautiously around the corner. As he ducked back toward Hans and Gretchen, his teeth were clenched in anger. "They're beating up an old man," he muttered. "Follow me."

The Jewish boy darted across the alley, through the backyards of several apartment buildings, and along the backside of a tall fence. He dropped to his knees in the tall weeds behind the fence and peered through the cracks between the planks. Hans and Gretchen caught up a moment later and crouched beside him. Miklös held one finger to his lips. "Look," he whispered.

Hans looked through a crack. One Arrow Cross tough held a young man at gunpoint while a second was beating an elderly man with a short wooden club. The old man was on his knees with his hands over his head, trying to protect his head from the blows. Blood dripped from his nose onto the bright yellow star on his chest.

"Please," the younger man begged, "have pity. Don't kill him. Beat me instead. Papa, let me take your place."

The *Nyala* with the club laughed. "You'll get your turn soon enough, dirty Jew swine!"

Rage flooded over Hans, but he was helpless to do anything. His heart went out to the two Jewish men.

"I'm gonna stop this," Miklös whispered. Snatching a thick wooden plank from the ground, he darted around the end of the fence to come up behind the youthful trooper with the gun. Miklös swung the plank with all his might, and the Arrow Cross man fell unconscious.

Moving with incredible speed, Miklös snatched the rifle from the youth's hands even before his body hit the ground. "Stop!" he screamed. "Leave that man alone."

The *Nyala* with the club spun around in astonishment. His gaze darted to his companion lying motionless on the ground and then back to the weapon in Miklös's hands. "Don't try it, Jew boy," he threatened. "We'll kill you."

"Not today," Miklös replied calmly. "Drop the club."

The *Nyala* started toward Miklös. "Give me the gun, Jew boy, or you're gonna be in big trouble."

Miklös fired a shot at the ground between the *Nyala's* feet, and the youth jumped back. "You don't know what you're doing, Jew boy," he threatened. "We'll kill you."

"Turn around," Miklös growled. "Now!"

The Arrow Cross youth raised his hands and turned around. "You kill me, and you're in big trouble," he blustered, but his voice trembled.

"I'm not gonna kill you," Miklös said scornfully, "but you're not gonna beat up a helpless old man." He turned to the young Jew, who by now was helping his father to his feet. "Move out of here as fast as you can," he whispered. "We'll keep them occupied until you have time to get away."

The young Jewish man nodded. "God's blessings upon you, friend, for helping us. They were killing Papa." He helped his father hurry away.

"Benjamin," Miklös said, addressing Hans, "there's a manhole in the middle of the alley behind us. See if you can get the cover open."

Hans found a large piece of scrap iron and used it to pry the heavy lid from the manhole. Grunting with the effort, he dragged the cover to one side.

"Gut!" Miklös said with satisfaction. He stepped forward and prodded the Arrow Cross youth with the muzzle of the rifle. "You. Walk backwards slowly."

The youth obeyed, shuffling backwards until he reached the open manhole. "Now," Miklös ordered, "step in."

The trooper hesitated.

"Go on," Miklös scoffed. "It's less than five meters deep. You're not gonna kill yourself."

"Jew boy, you're gonna regret this," the trooper snarled.

Miklös responded by firing another shot at the ground. "Now, coward! I'm losing patience."

The Arrow Cross youth stepped into the hole and disappeared from sight. Miklös dropped the rifle in the weeds at the edge of the alley. He ran back to where the unconscious *Nyala* lay. Gripping the youth by the wrists, Miklös dragged him to the manhole and slid him in feet first.

Hans helped Miklös replace the cover. "Let's get out of here," Miklös said, "before they figure their way out."

Hans, Gretchen, and Miklös arrived at Wallenberg's Ulloi Street office to find a huge crowd of Jews filling the yard and the street. "Let's cut through the alley," Hans suggested. "We'll never get in this way."

Wallenberg met them at the door. "I'm glad you're here," he told them. "We're being swamped with calls for help, and there's a lot to do. I'd like you to make some food deliveries for me."

Miklös stared out the window at the crowd in the yard. He beckoned to Wallenberg. "Sir, would you come and take a look at this woman?" he asked. "Did you ever see a more dejected human being?"

Wallenberg stepped to the window, and Hans and Gretchen squeezed in beside him. The humble diplomat put a gentle hand on each of their shoulders. "Always remember," he said softly, "that no matter how big your troubles are, there is always somebody with bigger troubles than yours. And when you help them, your own troubles seem to get smaller." He pointed through the window. "I dare say that woman's troubles are bigger than our own."

The woman was collapsed against the slats of the wooden fence outside the office window. Tears ran down her face. She held a baby in one arm; a small boy stood silently beside her.

Wallenberg cleared his throat. "Let's see if we can help her, shall we?" The three young assistants followed him from the office.

"What seems to be the trouble, little mother?" Wallenberg asked gently, laying a hand on the young woman's shoulder. The woman convulsed in sobs and, for several moments, could not even speak. Finally, she regained her composure enough to explain her predicament.

"We desperately need one of the *Schützpasses*," she sobbed, "but I'm afraid that the line is so long we will never get to the front before the curfew." She began to cry even harder. Her slender body shook as she wailed, "And we've been coming every day for a week! I'm afraid we'll never get a pass!"

Wallenberg patted the woman's shoulder. "Miklös, take the baby, would you?" he said. "Hans, you take the little fellow, and Gretchen, you help the lady. We'll just go inside and get this family their *Schützpasses* right now."

Fifteen minutes later, the young mother wept tears of gratitude as she slipped out the side door with the precious *Schützpasses* tucked inside her coat.

"Lars Berg just finished loading a cart for the safe houses on Kovarcz Street," Wallenberg told the young people. "We figure it has a better chance of making it past the Arrow Cross check points this way than if we attempt to take it by truck." He stepped to a large map on the wall. "Let me show you how to get to Kovarcz Street."

Miklös began to laugh, and the diplomat turned around. "What's so funny, Miklös?"

"I could find Kovarcz Street on the darkest night with my eyes closed!" Miklös snickered.

Wallenberg chuckled. "I forgot. I got used to showing Hans and Gretchen the various routes, and I guess I wasn't thinking about you being back in action." He gave Miklös an affectionate thump on the shoulder. "Welcome back, son."

He opened the back door. "Lars is ready for you. Be careful."

Miklös followed Hans and Gretchen to a walled-in yard behind the building. As they slipped through the gate, they found Lars Berg pulling a two-wheeled oxcart toward them. He slowed as he reached the gate.

Gretchen climbed up on one of the big wooden wheels and peered into the cart. "Manure?" she exclaimed. "We're delivering manure?"

Lars laughed. "It's good for the gardens, Gretchen."

Gretchen frowned. "I don't understand. We're going to risk our lives to deliver a load of manure?"

Lars laughed again. "You're actually delivering tins of powdered milk, rolled oats, fresh bread, and canned goods. There's a canvas tarp covering the foodstuffs, with a thin layer of manure over that. It's a bit unpleasant, but it may help you get past the Nazis and Arrow Cross. Who's going to stop you for a load of manure?"

Miklös nodded. "Not bad, Lars," he teased. "You're learning."

The man swung a playful punch at Miklös. "Get out of here, boy," he said with a grin. "You could learn a lot from me!"

Lars grew serious. "Be careful, all of you. If you are stopped, surrender the food if you have to. Better to lose the food than to lose your lives, too."

He stepped to the rear of the cart. "If you'll lift the tarp carefully from this end, you can unload the cases of food without too much trouble."

Lars looked at Miklös. "You're going to houses fifteen and sixteen. You know the contacts. Divide the load evenly between the two, but save two tins of oatmeal, two tins of milk, and two loaves of bread for the Mandl family living in the basement under the old library. Drop those items off in the usual place on your way back, and leave the cart behind the food cache off Harmincad Street."

Hans and Miklös took hold of the tongue and pulled the cart through the gate. Lars closed it behind them. "Be careful."

After delivering the food safely to the yellow star houses on Kovarcz Street, Hans, Gretchen, and Miklös headed for the old library with the remainder of the load.

"The manure idea worked well, didn't it?" Miklös remarked. "Nobody gave the cart a second glance."

Gretchen wrinkled her nose. *"Ja,"* she agreed, "but I hope they soon come up with a better idea. We're gonna smell like this stuff for a week."

"We just found out that Wallenberg has food warehoused in six different locations," Hans told Miklös, "three on the Buda side of the city, and three on the Pest side. The locations are top secret, of course, to keep them from falling into the hands of the Nazis or Arrow Cross. Wallenberg was smart enough to see what was coming, and he bought all the tins of food he could during September and early October. Lars told us he even uses the food to bribe the Arrow Cross into helping him save Jewish lives."

Miklös swung the tongue around and turned the oxcart down a side street. "Let's cut through Saint Gellert Park," he suggested. "That'll save us some walking."

When they reached the park, Hans and Gretchen pushed on the back of the cart to help Miklös get the wheels up over the curb, and they began to wheel the clumsy vehicle through an abandoned playground. A swing that had not seen use in many months sat rusting in a jungle of waist-high grass and weeds, while a forgotten slide, merry-go-round, and climbing bars stood forlornly nearby. Hans and Miklös struggled to wheel the cart through the tangles of weeds and briars.

"This place sure has been neglected, hasn't it?" Hans observed. "It's kind of sad."

Miklös shrugged. "Who's gonna bring their family to the park for a picnic when they might lose their lives before the outing's over?"

Gretchen stopped abruptly. "Sh-h-h," she whispered. "I heard something."

The three stood still, listening intently. Hans pointed at the tangle of vegetation blocking the path. "There. There's someone in there," he whispered.

Gretchen glanced nervously behind her. She and the boys were alone in the deserted park.

Suddenly, a man seemed to fall from behind a tree to land on his knees at Hans's feet. He was pitifully thin, with hollow, sunken eyes and a scraggly beard. The man's hair was matted and dirty, and his clothes were in tatters. He startled Hans by grabbing the boy's ankles with skeletal hands. "Please, help me," he whispered. "I must have food for my family. Please, can you—" A rattling cough interrupted his pitiful plea for help.

Miklös knelt and gently pried the man's fingers loose from Hans's clothing. He held both the man's hands to keep him from grabbing Hans again. "How can we help you, sir?"

"I'm begging you, son," the man implored him feebly. "We must have food. My wife is dying, but my children have to eat. We must have food for them."

Hans knelt beside the man. "What is your name, sir?"

"Benjamin Szekacs. Before the Nazis came, I owned the bakery on the Corso and the one on Tigris Street in Buda. When they came for us, we barely escaped with our lives."

"Where's your family?" Gretchen asked gently.

The man pointed to the tangled thicket. "We live in there. But there's no food, and I dare not leave my family to go in search of any."

Hans and Miklös glanced at each other. "What do you think?" Hans whispered. "Should we give him some of the food that was for the Mandl family?"

Miklös nodded. "Let's give him all of it. Wallenberg won't be upset. We'll get more for the Mandls."

Hans stood to his feet and peeled back the manure-spattered tarp. He grabbed two loaves of bread and a tin of powdered milk, and then knelt beside Mr. Szekacs. "We have food," he said softly.

The man's eyes grew wide. "Oh, my," he stammered. "Oh, my. Oh, my!"

"Mr. Szekacs, can you show us where your family is?" Miklös asked.

The man nodded. He turned and crawled under the edge of the thicket. Miklös grabbed a tin of oatmeal from the cart and handed it to Gretchen, then grabbed the remaining tins of milk and oatmeal himself. Hans, Miklös, and Gretchen crawled through the thicket, dragging the food items with them.

After crawling five or six meters, they came upon a scene that brought tears to Gretchen's eyes. A terribly emaciated woman was lying on the ground in a tiny space that had been cleared beneath the bushes. She was wrapped in a blanket, with five thin, dirty children seated around her. The woman didn't move as they approached, but five pairs of large, sad eyes watched them carefully.

Hans glanced upward and saw that a large, green tarpaulin had been carefully fastened to the branches to form a makeshift roof over the burrowlike area. He shook his head sadly.

"We have food, children!" Mr. Szekacs exclaimed. "These good people have brought us food!"

Hans ripped the paper wrapper from a loaf of bread, and the children's eyes grew wide. He tore a large chunk from the loaf and handed it to the nearest child, who took it timidly, as if the gift were too good to be true. Moving as fast as he could, Hans distributed the bread to all five children. Watching the starving children stuff the bread into their mouths, Gretchen began to cry.

Hans tore a large chunk from the loaf and handed it to Mr. Szekacs, who shook his head. "It's for the children," the man whispered.

Hans held the bread out toward him. "*Nein,* Herr Szekacs, you must take some. There's more where this came from." He slid one of the tins toward the starving man. "We have milk, and we have oatmeal, and tomorrow we can bring beans and more bread and canned vegetables."

Tears flowed down the man's cheeks. He crawled over to the silent form on the ground and stroked his wife's hair. "We have food, Maria," he wept. "Can you hear me? We have food."

The woman stirred and opened her eyes. "Benjamin, where are the children? Who has taken my children?"

"They're right here, my love," Benjamin Szekacs answered. "They're eating bread, Maria! We have food!" He held one of the tins where she could see it. "There's milk and bread and oatmeal. We have food!"

Hans used his knife to pry the lid from one of the tins of powdered milk. "Hold out your hands," he told the nearest child. The boy cupped his hands, and Hans carefully poured a white mound of milk powder into them. A warm feeling of satisfaction swept over Hans as he watched the boy devour the dried milk.

Hans, Gretchen, and Miklös sat side by side and watched as the hungry family consumed the entire tin of milk and the one of oatmeal. Mr. Szekacs fed bits of bread and handfuls of milk powder to his wife. "Can we have more bread, Papa?" a tiny voice asked, but Mr. Szekacs shook his head. "Let's save the other loaf for tomorrow," he replied.

Hans placed the second loaf of bread in Mr. Szekacs's hands. "Go ahead," he urged the man. "We'll bring more tomorrow."

As Hans knelt beside the man, he suddenly felt tiny arms around his neck and looked over to see a tiny sprite of a girl beside him. A huge mass of tight curls framed a thin, dirty face, but the smile was radiant. "Thank you," the little tyke said softly in Magyar. "You are good. The men with guns are bad, but you are good!"

Mr. Szekacs looked up from his task of distributing the second loaf of bread. "This is Hannah," he said proudly. "She's four."

Hans reached over and tousled the thick curls. "*Guten tag,* Hannah," he said softly. "My name is Hans." The tiny arms around his neck squeezed tight as the little girl gave him a second hug.

"Benjamin is nine," Mr. Szekacs continued, "Liesl is seven, Ivan is six, and little Rachelle is two." His eyes welled up again with tears. "Thank you for saving my children's lives."

"We'll bring more food tomorrow," Hans promised. He gave little Hannah a hug and then followed Gretchen and Miklös as they crawled from the hideaway shelter.

"What a sad situation," Hans remarked as he and Miklös pushed and pulled the oxcart across the park. "Imagine. Seven people living like animals under the bushes!"

"It's a terrible place to live," Gretchen agreed. "But at least we can bring them food."

"We'll do more than that," Miklös promised. "That woman needs a doctor. As soon as we tell Wallenberg about her, I know he'll send a car to take her to one of his hospitals. Let's hurry!"

As the cart rolled smoothly down Csepel Street, the roar of aircraft engines made them all look up. A squadron of Russian bombers passed overhead. "More death and destruction," Miklös sighed. "I just hope this war gets over before Budapest is reduced to a pile of rubble." The whistle of bombs and explosions rumbling close by caused the Hungarian boy to wince.

A command shouted in Magyar made them all spin around. Three grinning *Nyalis* with automatic rifles strode briskly toward them. Hans's heart sank. One of the troopers was the girl from the bridge.

"Glad to see me?" the Arrow Cross girl sneered at Hans. She leveled her rifle at him. "Now we finish what we started the other day. This time, there will be no interruptions."

CHAPTER NINE
THE GIFT

The Arrow Cross girl turned to her two companions. "The blond fellow is mine," she said. "You can have the skinny one and the girl."

"Let's take all three to the river," one of the others suggested. "We each shoot one."

The girl shook her head. "We do it right here, right now," she insisted. "I'm not going to waste any time or take any chances. We're going to shoot them right now!"

Their victims looked from one *Nyala* to another in panic. "Wait!" Miklös cried out. "Spare us. We can get you food. We can—"

"Stow it!" the Arrow Cross girl snapped. "We've wasted enough time for talk already." She gestured with the muzzle of her rifle toward the narrow space between two abandoned buildings. "In there. March!"

"Please," Gretchen begged. "You don't have to do this. It doesn't matter to you if we live or die. So why not let us live?"

"Enough talk," the girl growled. She gestured again toward the narrow court. "Now march. *Mach schnell!*"

Miklös, Hans, and Gretchen slowly trudged into the gap between the two brick buildings. An unusual peace flooded over Hans. "This isn't in their hands," he whispered to Gretchen. "They can only kill us if God allows it. If it's not our time, He'll stop them."

Gretchen shook her head. "There's no way out of this, Hans. Did you see the hatred in that girl's eyes?"

They passed beneath an iron fire escape running up to the second and third floors. Hans glanced up at it, and the Arrow Cross girl noticed. "Go ahead, try it," she jeered. "Do you think you can climb faster than a bullet?"

The court ended with a brick wall less than ten meters from the sidewalk. There was no place to go, no place to run. *Lord, help us,* Hans prayed silently.

Hans glanced over at Gretchen and saw the fear etched upon her face. Miklös was trembling.

"Against the wall," the girl ordered. "Turn around and face us."

"Please," Miklös begged, falling to his knees. "Please. Don't do this."

The girl laughed and turned to her companions, who stood on each side of her with their guns leveled at Hans, Miklös, and Gretchen. "This is rather amusing, don't you think?" she taunted. "All my life I've been ordered around. Do this. Don't do that. It's kind of nice to hear someone saying please. And you know what makes it even better? It's a dirty Jew doing the begging."

She took a step into the alley. "Jew boy, my friends and I really don't want to kill you. But we have to. You and your kind have—" Her words were drowned out by the roar of low-flying aircraft, and she stopped and glanced upward. She raised her rifle to her shoulder.

A deafening blast shattered the stillness as the building to the girl's left exploded in a barrage of flying bricks, timbers, and glass. The shock wave slammed Hans, Gretchen, and Miklös against the back wall of the alley. They landed in a crumpled heap as the fire escape came twisting and snapping down upon them, striking the pavement less than a meter from where they lay. With a roar, the wall on the other side collapsed into the alley. The ground shook with the explosion as bricks and debris rained down around them. Another section of the fire escape came crashing down to land on top of the first. Dust filled the air.

Stunned by the blast, Hans lay quietly for a moment and then managed to lift his head. "Gretchen, are you all right?"

"I-I think so," came the weak reply.

"Miklös?"

"If you'll get off me, I think I'm still alive," the Jewish boy answered.

Stunned and shaken, Hans got to his knees. Gretchen was sitting up with a dazed look on her face, and Miklös was holding his head. Coughing and choking, they crawled from beneath the mangled fire escape to stand shakily to their feet.

"Oh, my," Gretchen exclaimed, as they stood surveying the damage. "What happened?"

The alley was buried beneath a mound of bricks nearly two meters high. A twisted steel beam protruded upwards at a rakish angle, and a mangled section of the fire escape rested on top of the rubble.

"Russian bomb," Miklös said matter-of-factly. "That building took a direct hit."

"The *Nyalis!*" Gretchen exclaimed. Her hand flew to her mouth.

"They're gone," Hans said. He shook his head. "It was their time, not ours. God's timing is never wrong."

Miklös gave him a strange look.

They climbed carefully over the pile of debris and emerged back on the street. "Let's get out of here," Miklös urged, "in case another squad of Arrow Cross was attracted by the blast. They'd try to blame the whole thing on us." They hurried down a side street.

"Your head is bleeding, Hans," Gretchen observed. "You're hurt."

Hans reached up and felt the back of his head. His fingers came away sticky with blood. "Here, sit down for a second," Miklös advised, pointing to a low wall that ran parallel to the sidewalk. "Let me take a look at it."

Hans sank to a seat on the wall, and Miklös sat beside him. Gingerly, he parted Hans's hair and leaned close for a better look. "It's a bad scrape and it's bleeding a lot, but I don't think it's serious," Miklös decided. "Why don't you head home and clean it up?"

"We have to tell Wallenberg about the Szekacs family," Hans protested, "so he can get Mrs. Szekacs to the hospital."

"I'll go," Miklös replied. "You two go on home and take care of that injury." He pointed at Gretchen's right leg. "You've got a nasty scrape, too, Gretchen. Better get that cleaned up."

Miklös stood to his feet. "I'll get the food for the Mandl family and make sure that Wallenberg knows about the Szekacs family so we can get Mrs. Szekacs to one of his hospitals."

Papa sighed deeply as Hans and Gretchen finished telling him the story of their close encounter with the *Nyalis*. He bit his lip and shook his head. Hans could tell that their account of the ordeal was troubling him.

"Papa," Hans said quickly, "we were in God's hands the entire time. That Arrow Cross girl meant to kill us, but God stopped her. One moment she's pointing her rifle at me, and I figure I have less than five seconds to live. The next thing I know, we're all being knocked backwards by the bomb blast, and bricks and timbers are falling all around us. All three *Nyalis* were killed when the building collapsed on them."

Papa frowned as he thought it over. He let out his breath in a long, troubled sigh. "You're right, son," he said finally. "I can't ask you to stop helping Wallenberg because your lives are in danger. These are perilous times for everyone, and we have to trust the Lord."

Mr. Semestyen leaned forward. "When you think about it," he said, "we're all in danger, nearly every moment of the day. Danger from the Nazis, from the Arrow Cross, and from Allied bombs and artillery. I suppose the only safe place to be right now is one of the neutral countries." He shook his head. "That's what amazes me about Wallenberg. He's from Sweden, right? Sweden is neutral . . . a safe place! But Wallenberg, even though he's from a wealthy, powerful family, chooses to come to war-torn Hungary to help my people. What an unselfish human being."

Papa smiled. "All right, Herr Semestyen, I get your point. We all need to help others when we can, and I'll not deny Hans and Gretchen that opportunity."

He stood to his feet. "I'll be right back."

A moment later Papa returned to the tiny room with a small parcel, which he handed to Gretchen. "Here. I hope you like it."

Gretchen looked up in surprise. "What is it?"

Papa toyed with the end of his mustache. "It's your birthday present."

Gretchen was puzzled. "Papa, my birthday is more than two months away! This is only November."

Papa nodded soberly. "*Ja,* so it is." He smiled sadly. "But I have no guarantee that I'll be around in January, or that any of us will, for that matter. As we were just discussing, life is very fragile and uncertain, especially at a time such as this."

He gestured toward the package. "Go ahead, open it up. I want to see if you like it."

Gretchen tore the plain brown paper open to discover a brightly colored scarf. The pattern was woven in bold yellows, reds, and purples, creating a bright, cheery effect. Gretchen's eyes lit up when she saw it. "Papa, it's beautiful!"

"I found it in a shop just a few days ago," Papa told her, "and I immediately thought of you. It looks like something you would wear when you're cheerful and happy, and I thought that perhaps it would take your mind off the war. I'm sorry it's not something nicer."

Gretchen jumped up and gave him a hug. "It's wonderful, Papa. Thank you. I'll wear it every day." She flipped the scarf over her blond braids and quickly tied a knot under her chin. "How do I look?"

Papa grinned. "Like a princess."

"It's very pretty," Mr. Semestyen agreed. "You'll turn the head of every young fellow on the street."

Hans frowned. "That might not be such a good idea," he remarked. "At a time like this, a person wants to attract as little attention as possible. Papa, the scarf is pretty . . . but . . . do you think that maybe it's too bright? Considering the situation right now in Budapest, I mean."

Papa eyed the scarf thoughtfully. "You have a point, Hans," he agreed. "That's something I hadn't even considered."

"Save it," Mr. Semestyen suggested. "This war will not last forever. The Russians will be here soon, and life will soon return to normal. Then it will be safe to wear that beautiful scarf—anywhere!"

Gretchen studied her reflection in the tiny mirror beside the door. "The scarf is lovely, Papa, and I hate to put it away for later."

She spun around to face the others. "I'm going to wear it right away. Tomorrow. But I'll just wear it under my coat—around my neck—so that no one else will see it. Is that all right, Papa?"

Papa nodded. "*Ja,* that should be safe enough. Happy birthday, sweetheart. But remember, your birthday doesn't come for two more months. So don't start acting like an arrogant twelve-year-old until January."

Gretchen laughed and kissed him on the cheek. "Papa. Do you think I'm arrogant?"

Her father grinned. "Not yet," he replied, "but then, you're only eleven now."

She wrinkled her nose at him.

Hans laughed. "Happy birthday, Gretchen. That is a beautiful scarf."

Miklös was waiting in the repair shop when Hans and Gretchen came downstairs the next morning. "*Guten tag,* Gretchen, Hans," he said, addressing them in German.

Gretchen showed Miklös the birthday scarf. "What do you think? Papa gave it to me."

"It's colorful," the Jewish boy replied. He watched as Gretchen tucked the colorful scarf under her coat. "But why are you hiding it?"

"Hans thinks it's safer that way," Gretchen told him, "you know, so I don't attract attention from the *Nyalis* or the Nazis."

Miklös nodded. "That's good thinking."

He slapped his hat upon his head and buttoned his coat.

"Let's head over to Wallenberg's apartment. I'm supposed to take the Szekacs to one of the yellow star houses on Ulloi Street."

Hans was puzzled. "Wallenberg's apartment?" he echoed.

Miklös nodded. "Wallenberg took Mrs. Szekacs to one of his Jewish hospitals," he explained, "and since it was so late, he took the rest of the family to his place."

Ten minutes later the door to Wallenberg's apartment opened at Miklös's secret knock. "Come in," Mr. Szekacs greeted them. "We've been waiting for you."

The Szekacs children gathered around Miklös, Hans, and Gretchen as they entered the apartment. Hans noticed that the children were dressed in clothing that was much too big for them, but they were clean. They were bright and cheerful and seemed so different from the huddling, pitiful creatures of yesterday.

"Hans!" Little Hannah came flying across the room and leaped into his arms. Hans picked her up, and she wrapped her arms around his neck. "Papa gave me a bath, Hans. In Mr. Wallenberg's bathtub. And we got to sleep on real blankets. And we had food! Lots of it!"

Hans laughed and tousled her curls. "What did you have for supper?" he asked.

"Beans," the little girl replied with enthusiasm. "And cabbage and bread. As much as we could eat. It was wonderful."

A lump formed in Hans's throat as his mind went back to the crude shelter in Saint Gellert Park. "I'm glad you got to come here," he told her.

Mr. Szekacs was clean-shaven and dressed in faded but clean work clothes. His hair was neatly combed, and his eyes had lost their desperate, hopeless look. “Thank you, Miklös, Gretchen, Hans, for what you did for my family. We will never forget you as long as we live.” The man’s eyes filled with tears. “May God in heaven grant you sunshine on your path.”

Mr. Szekacs wiped his eyes with the back of his hand and looked hopefully at Miklös. “Any news about my wife?”

Miklös shook his head. “Not yet,” he replied, “but I’ll try to get a report on her this morning. Right now we’re supposed to take you to a yellow star house on Ulloi Street.”

Mr. Szekacs called the children together and helped them into the oversized coats that Wallenberg had managed to provide for them. “We’re ready,” he announced.

“I’m ready, too,” Hannah declared, extending her arms to Hans to be picked up. “Papa says we’re going to a new house.”

“Ja,” Hans agreed, holding the little girl close, “but I’ll warn you, there will be a lot of other people in your new house. You’ll have to share with everybody.”

Miklös led the way to the yellow star house while Hans and Hannah brought up the rear. As the little procession trooped across the intersection at Rakoczi Avenue, three Nazi officers stepped from the front door of the hotel on the corner.

“The Jewish situation is under control,” a tall, dignified officer was saying. “Eichmann has Vajna’s government and the local Gendarmes under his thumb. The trains are running to Auschwitz again, and the final pogrom is planned for the first week of December. The Jews are concentrated for the most part in the Central Ghetto and the International Ghetto, and they’re all marked with yellow stars. When the time comes, it will be a simple matter of—”

The Nazi stopped in mid-sentence as his attention was drawn to the Szekacs family. “You there,” he bellowed, addressing Mr. Szekacs, “aren’t you Jewish? Answer me, man!”

Mr. Szekacs was terrified. His eyes bulged, and his lips trembled as he attempted to answer, but no sound came out. His face turned white, and he looked as though he would pass out.

“Thought so,” the Nazi snarled. “And so are all these children, I’ll warrant.” He stepped forward and yanked the hat from Miklös’ head. “A Jewish dog if I ever saw one.”

The Nazi towered over Mr. Szekacs. “Where are your yellow stars, you miserable Jews? And why are you breaking curfew?” The Jewish man trembled.

Hans turned and attempted to casually walk away with Hannah but stopped abruptly as he heard the metallic click of someone cocking a pistol. He turned to see a large automatic in the officer’s hand. “You’re not going anywhere, *knabe,*” the man laughed. “Take off your hat.”

Hans complied with a shaking hand.

The Nazi studied Hans’s features and then turned on Gretchen. “You too, *fraulein*. Take off your hat.” Gretchen obeyed meekly.

The Nazi frowned. “You two are as Aryan as you can be. But you’re in the company of these vile Jews, and you’re obviously helping them, which is a crime.”

He gestured with his hand. “Winkelmann!”

One of the other officers stepped forward. “I want these prisoners taken to Bekasmegyer. All of them. They’ll be on the next train to Auschwitz.”

The two junior officers reached into their greatcoats and drew pistols. “You heard the officer,” Winkelmann barked. “March!”

CHAPTER TEN

THE DEATH MARCH

"I just wasn't thinking!" Miklös berated himself as he, Hans, and Gretchen were led away with the Szekacs family. "We should have gone through the lower city. With all the German patrols and *Nyalis* about, we were bound to run into trouble, but I just wasn't thinking. This is all my fault."

"*Nein,* not really," Hans replied in a whisper. "We just walked into a trap. Our attention was on the Szekacs children, and we weren't paying attention. I'm as much to blame as—"

"Silence!" the officer named Winkelmann ordered, and Hans fell silent.

The Nazis marched them a few short blocks to the Arrow Cross headquarters. Hans felt a chill of horror as they entered the building. Many a Jew had been tortured to death inside the walls of this very building. He glanced at Gretchen and realized that she was more afraid than he was. He prayed silently for her.

"Lock them up," Winkelmann told the Arrow Cross trooper at the front desk, "but not with the other Jews. Veesenmayer wants us to escort them personally to Bekasmegyer so there's no chance for escape. I'll send SS troops for them this afternoon."

Veesenmayer! Hans's heart jumped at the name. They had been captured by none other than Edmund Veesenmayer, one of the highest-ranking officers in the Third Reich!

Three green Tiger tanks and two blue armored personnel carriers rumbled past the Arrow Cross headquarters that afternoon as four youthful Nazis led Miklös, Hans, Gretchen, and the Szekacs family down the front steps. "Where are they taking us, Papa?" seven-year-old Liesl asked fearfully.

"I don't know, Liesl," her father replied.

"Are they going to hurt us?"

"I don't know, sweetheart."

"Silence!" one of the soldiers ordered, reaching out to slap Liesl on the side of the head. Tears filled the little girl's eyes, but she didn't make a sound.

The soldiers marched them to Erzsebert Square, where they joined hundreds of condemned Jews. Hans looked about desperately for a way to escape, but the SS soldiers stayed close, as if they were anticipating his attempt. Several hundred more Jews were driven into the square, and then the march to the Bekasmegyer brickyard began.

Hans, Miklös, and Mr. Szekacs took turns carrying Hannah and little Rachelle, while Gretchen tried to help and encourage the other three children. Hans watched the Jews around him as they marched, noticing with sorrow the dejected slump to their shoulders, the vacant stare, and the listless movements of their limbs. *These people have simply given up,* he told himself. *They wouldn't try to escape even if they were given half a chance.*

Hunger, thirst, fatigue, and fear plagued Hans and the others as the long march continued. Hans shifted Rachelle to his other arm. The afternoon was so cold. *If only they would give us a chance to stop and rest.* But the soldiers and Arrow Cross had already shot several stragglers, and Hans forced himself to keep moving. He caught Gretchen's eye and gave her a gentle smile.

They reached Bekasmegyer late that afternoon. The guards cursed and struck at the marchers as they drove them into the desolate brickyard. Hans felt a wave of hopelessness as he surveyed the area. *This is where we made the rescue*, he thought, *and now there's nobody to rescue us.*

Hans, Gretchen, and Miklös somehow managed to keep the Szekacs family together as the abusive guards drove the hordes of condemned Jews through the brickyard gates. "Over there," Miklös said, pointing to one of the huge brick kilns. "If we can find a place against the wall, it will afford us a tiny bit of shelter."

Hans sank wearily to the ground with his back against the rough stone wall of the kiln. Gretchen dropped in beside him, and Miklös found a place on his other side. Mr. Szekacs sagged to a spot beside Gretchen, and his children huddled fearfully around him. Hannah climbed into Hans's lap.

"Attention!" a harsh voice blared through a bullhorn, and the weary marchers looked up to see an Arrow Cross guard standing on one of the loading platforms. "There will be no escape attempts," the guard bellowed. "If anyone tries, we will machine-gun the entire group!"

Gretchen shuddered.

"There's no hope for us now," Miklös muttered despondently. "Even Wallenberg doesn't know we are here, about to be shipped to Auschwitz."

"God knows where we are," Hans said softly.

Miklös gave him a reproachful look. "God?" he echoed. "What does God have to do with it? He doesn't even care what happens to us." The Hungarian boy gestured toward the sea of helpless humanity about him. "These are my people, Hans. And sometime in the next few days, we're all going to die—just because we're Jews!" Miklös clenched his fist. "But God doesn't care, and Wallenberg can't help us because he doesn't know."

"But God does care," Hans protested. "He does! He's our hope, not Herr Wallenberg."

"Then why don't you pray and ask God to send Wallenberg to get us out of here?" Miklös replied bitterly.

The directness of the challenge stunned Hans. Would God send Wallenberg to their rescue if Hans asked Him? He swallowed hard. His faith in God was very real, and yet, this was perhaps the greatest test of faith he had ever faced. Knowing that Miklös was watching him, Hans bowed his head. He decided to pray aloud.

"Father," he prayed earnestly, "You know where we are and that we are facing deportation to the death camp at Auschwitz. Miklös doesn't believe that You can do it, but I'm asking You to somehow send Wallenberg or one of the men from the other neutral legations to our rescue. Father, we don't have much time until the death trains come for us, so please, help us quickly. In Jesus' name I ask it, Amen."

Hans opened his eyes to see Miklös shaking his head scornfully.

Little Hannah reached up with a tiny hand to stroke the side of Hans's face. "Will God tell Mr. Wallenberg to come get us?" she asked. Hans smiled at her without answering.

Hans turned to Miklös. "There's something I've been wanting to ask you ever since Gretchen and I first met you," he said. "Miklös, are you a Christian? Have you ever been saved?"

Miklös snorted. "A Christian? Why would I want to be a Christian?" He pointed to the SS soldiers and the Arrow Cross troops who were strutting about the brickyard with their automatic weapons. "It's Christians who are killing my people."

Hans was stunned by Miklös's reply. "Those aren't Christians," he protested.

"They're not Jews," Miklös shot back.

Hans sighed. "Miklös," he said, "people aren't Christians just because they're non-Jewish. They're Gentiles. People become Christians only when they ask Jesus Christ to forgive their sins and become their Savior."

He gestured toward the Nazis and Arrow Cross with a nod of his head. "I can tell you this, Miklös, those men are not Christians. A follower of Jesus would never kill or persecute innocent Jews. These guards are not Jewish, but that doesn't make them Christians. They are Gentiles!"

"What about Father Kun?" Miklös argued. "They say that he attends the Arrow Cross executions just to see Jews die. He raises his crucifix in the air and calls, 'In the holy name of Jesus, fire!' " Miklös clenched his teeth. "You can't tell me that he's not a Christian. He's a follower of Christ!"

Hans shook his head vehemently. "Father Kun is not a Christian, Miklös. He's a religious man, but he's a follower of a religious system, not a follower of Christ. A true Christian is a person who has received Jesus as his Savior by faith, and I know that Father Kun has never done that."

Miklös frowned. "Are you telling me," he asked, "that religious people are not really Christians? What's the difference?"

Hans shook his head and moved Hannah to the other side of his lap. "Religion doesn't save anybody," he said softly. "Budapest is filled with churches that teach that salvation comes by doing good deeds or by religious ceremonies through the church. But the Bible doesn't teach that, and it's not God's way to heaven."

"Then what is God's way?" Miklös asked.

"The Bible teaches that we all are sinners," Hans replied. "Romans 3:23 says 'For all have sinned, and come short of the glory of God.' Because we are sinners, we can't go to heaven, unless we get forgiveness from our sins."

"How can we do that?" the Jewish boy asked.

"Jesus Christ died on the cross so that our sins could be forgiven," Hans answered. "He arose from the dead the third day and now offers salvation as a free gift. Romans 5:8 tells us: 'But God commendeth his love toward us, in that, while we were yet sinners, Christ died for us.' When a person asks Jesus to be his Savior, his sin and guilt are transferred to Christ, and he is forgiven forever."

Miklös frowned. "So all you have to do is ask?"

"Believe and ask," Hans replied. "There's another verse in the Book of Romans that promises, 'For whosoever shall call upon the name of the Lord shall be saved.' If you'll repent of your sins, believe that Jesus died for you and rose again, and ask Him by faith to save you, the Bible promises that He'll save you. It's that easy."

Miklös shook his head. "That's not the way I was taught," he replied, "and I could never betray my people."

"It's not betrayal," Hans insisted. "Jesus came as your Messiah! He offers you salvation as a gift if you'll simply receive Him by faith and ask Him to save you."

Mr. Szekacs leaned across Gretchen. "Don't talk anymore," he whispered urgently. "The Arrow Cross guards seem very nervous, and they're beating anybody who gives them the slightest excuse."

Hans nodded. "I think you're right." He sighed as he leaned back against the rough stonework of the kiln. "We're in for a long night."

CHAPTER ELEVEN
DIFFICULT DECISION

The temperature dropped quickly as the evening sun sank behind the hills overlooking Budapest. A cold wind gusted and howled, driving a chilling rain across the Bekasmegyer brickyard and causing the helpless captives to huddle closer together. They wrapped their tattered garments even tighter about themselves in a futile attempt to stay warm. The guards built several fires between the drying sheds but used their rifle butts against any Jews who dared to venture close to the blazing fires for warmth.

Hans felt a growing sense of dread as he watched the November twilight descend on the brickyard. *What if God doesn't deliver us this time? What if He allows us to be taken to Auschwitz? It's happened to countless Jews, and it's even happened to other Christians!* He slipped an arm around Gretchen and pulled her close as he breathed a silent prayer for courage and strength. Gretchen looked up at him and smiled bravely through her tears.

Dear God, Hans cried silently, *please protect her from harm.*

Hans suddenly became aware of the fact that Miklös was shaking his arm vigorously. "Hans, look," the Jewish boy exclaimed again, "look who's here!"

A blue Studebaker sped through the gates of the brickyard, followed by two large trucks. "Wallenberg," Hans breathed in astonishment. "Thank You, Lord Jesus."

Hans turned to Miklös in delight. "God answered my prayer already," he whispered. "I'll try to work my way through the crowd and let him know that we're here."

A barrage of automatic weapon fire echoed across the brickyard, and Hans spun around to see an Arrow Cross man standing atop a loading dock. "Stay where you are," the man shouted across the sea of cowering prisoners. "Anyone who moves will be shot!"

Hans's heart pounded with terror as he crawled and pushed his way through the huddled masses of condemned Jews, slowly working his way toward Wallenberg's Studebaker. He froze in position every time the guard on the dock looked in his direction. Less than fifteen meters from the Studebaker, he paused in frustration. Hundreds and hundreds of condemned Jews huddled on the ground between him and the auto. There would be no way to push his way through without attracting the attention of the guards. Finally, Hans crawled around the densest part of the crowd, under one of the trucks, and out from underneath to reach the vicinity of the Studebaker.

Wallenberg was arguing with an angry group of SS officers. One of the Nazis held a revolver against the diplomat's side, but Wallenberg appeared not to even notice it. "You are breaking international law!" Wallenberg screamed in fluent German, jumping up and down. "Many of these people have protective passports, and you cannot take them. I will not let you. You are breaking international law, and I will hold you responsible."

The Nazi with the revolver struck Wallenberg sharply in the side with the weapon, and Wallenberg grunted in pain. Slowly, deliberately, the officer pointed the gun directly at Wallenberg's chest. "Take your trucks and your men," he ordered, "and leave this instant. If you do not, I will shoot you down right here!"

Hans held his breath. "Protect him, Lord," he prayed desperately.

Wallenberg calmly raised his hands. Slowly, carefully, he reached inside his coat and withdrew a sheaf of papers. "I have orders from General Schmidthuber," he shouted at the Nazi with the revolver, "and you will not stand in my way. You are to release five hundred of these prisoners to me immediately."

The SS officer seized the papers, glanced briefly at them, and then thrust them back at the diplomat. "Only those with *Schütz-passes,*" he thundered, "and we will be checking. If you attempt to take any without passes, we will shoot them on the spot."

Hans stepped forward. "Herr Wallenberg."

Wallenberg glanced in Hans's direction, and his face registered his surprise. "Hans," he exclaimed, "what are you doing here?"

"Gretchen and Miklös are here, too," Hans replied breathlessly, "and the Szekacs family. We were taken prisoner and marched here this afternoon."

"Vilmos," Wallenberg called, "get two of the men and follow Hans. I want the Szekacs family on the first truck, and I want Hans, Gretchen, and Miklös in the auto. But hurry!"

Ten minutes later, Hans waited as Gretchen and Miklös scrambled into the back seat of the Studebaker. The Szekacs family was safely aboard one of the Red Cross trucks. As Hans leaned down to enter the car, the Nazi that had challenged Wallenberg stepped forward. "Just a minute, *knabe,*" he growled, pointing his revolver at Hans. "Where's your *Schützpasse?*"

Hans looked up in panic. "I-I don't have it," he stammered. "But I'm not Jewish."

"Then you don't go, do you?" the Nazi growled. "Only those with passes."

Wallenberg came striding over. "The boy goes with me," he said in an authoritative voice.

"He doesn't have a *Schützpasse,*" the Nazi said firmly. "He stays here."

"He's on my personal staff," Wallenberg argued. "He and his sister are couriers for the legation."

"I don't care who he is or what he does for the legation," the officer replied impatiently. "He doesn't have a *Schützpasse*. If you try to take him, I will shoot him right here."

"Hans, get in the car," Wallenberg ordered.

Hans hesitated.

"Get in the car, now," Wallenberg repeated.

The Nazi aimed the revolver at Hans's chest. "If you do, *knabe,* you're dead."

In terror, Hans looked at Wallenberg. "Get in, Hans," the diplomat said again. "He can't stop you."

The Nazi officer raised the revolver so that it now pointed at Hans's face. "Take one more step toward that auto, and I'll blast you into eternity," he growled.

Hans realized that he was facing the most difficult decision of his entire life. His heart raced, and his breath came in short, trembling gasps. *Lord Jesus,* he prayed frantically, *help me.*

Wallenberg stepped closer. "You shoot the boy and you'll answer directly to General Schmidthuber," he said quietly. "I'll make sure of that personally." In the same calm, quiet tone, he ordered, "Hans, get into the car."

With limbs stiffened by fear, Hans slowly stepped into the car, fully expecting the burning pain of a Nazi bullet as he did. As Hans sank into the plush fabric of the rear seat, Wallenberg closed the door. Hans turned slightly.

The Nazi officer was gone.

CHAPTER TWELVE

EICHMANN'S DEATH MARCHES

"Eichmann no longer has access to the Hungarian trains," Wallenberg told them as the Studebaker sped along behind the two Red Cross trucks. "They're needed for the war effort. If we had not come in time, you would have been marched to the border at Hegyeshalom, and from there to a train for the death camp at Strasshof or Auschwitz. It would have been a long, brutal march, I'm afraid."

"But Veesenmayer said that the death trains were running again," Miklös remarked.

"They were until two days ago," Wallenberg replied, "but Himmler has requisitioned all of them for the war effort. Eichmann can't get a single train right now. But it's not going to stop him from killing Jews; he's simply going to march them to their deaths."

"We're thankful you came when you did," Hans said quietly. He leaned forward. "But how did you get five hundred into just two trucks?"

Wallenberg sighed. "We didn't, Hans. I'm afraid we rescued less than two hundred."

Hans was puzzled. "But why didn't you bring more trucks?" he questioned. "If General Schmidthuber granted you permission to take five hundred, you knew it would take more than two trucks."

Wallenberg laughed. "Those papers were more than a month old, Hans. And I've already used them on several other occasions."

Hans chuckled.

Wallenberg sighed. "If I had had any idea what we'd find in the brickyard, I would have brought several more trucks. I just came on a hunch, and I really didn't have the heart to ask the Red Cross for more than two trucks."

"So you didn't know that any Jews were at the brickyard?" The question came from Miklös.

"No," Wallenberg answered, "or I would have brought more trucks."

"So no one called or sent you a message?"

"No."

Miklös leaned forward. "Then why did you come?"

Wallenberg shrugged. "I'm not really sure, Miklös," he answered slowly. "I just had this strange feeling that I ought to check out the brickyard. When I mentioned it to Vilmos, he agreed to come with me, so I called for two trucks and brought several staff members along. To tell you the truth, I'm still not sure why we came, but I'm thankful we did."

Miklös glanced at Hans and then looked away quickly. Hans knew exactly what he was thinking.

As the trucks slowed for the turn into Erzsebert Square, a young man leaped into the headlights of the Studebaker. He jumped up and down, waving his arms wildly.

"Stop the car," Wallenberg told Vilmos, "it's Johnny Moser."

The young man ran forward as the car slowed to a stop. "We've been looking all over for you," he told Wallenberg, who had rolled down the window. "We have three trucks of food and medical supplies to distribute to the Jews who are on the death march to Hegyeshalom, as well as several doctors and nurses that are willing to go. Will you go along and help us try to rescue as many marchers as we can?"

Wallenberg sighed wearily. "Of course I'll go," he said quietly. "Where do we meet the trucks?"

"They're waiting for us at the legation."

Wallenberg glanced toward the three young people in the back seat. "We need to take Hans, Gretchen, and Miklös home, then we'll meet you there." He paused thoughtfully. "Hans, I know it's a lot to ask, but I don't know anyone better with a camera than you. Would you be willing to go?"

Hans nodded.

Moments later the Studebaker pulled up in front of Mr. Semestyen's repair shop, and Gretchen and Miklös scrambled out. "You don't need to take me home," Miklös said. "If you'll lend me a light, I can get home safely through the lower city. That will save you some time."

Vilmos handed Miklös a flashlight, and the Jewish boy disappeared around the corner of the building. Gretchen hurried into the safety of the shop.

Rain mixed with sleet spattered the windshield of the Studebaker as Vilmos pulled out of the alley behind the Swedish Legation. Headlights illuminated the interior of the car as the first cattle truck in the caravan swung into position behind them. Hans looked back to see two other trucks turn into the street, followed by a single automobile. He knew that all three trucks contained food and medical supplies and that the car was carrying several doctors and nurses.

"Hans, this is Tom Veres," Wallenberg was saying. "He's joined our staff as my official photographer. Tom, this is Hans Von Edler, and he's also quite handy with a camera. I want both of you to shoot as many photos as you can on this trip."

Hans leaned forward and shook hands with Tom, who was seated in the front beside Vilmos. "Good to meet another shutterbug," the stocky young photographer said, returning the handshake. Wavy brown hair framed a handsome face and a friendly grin, and Hans liked the young Jewish man immediately.

"I'm really not a photographer," Hans explained, "but I shot a few photos the other day, and Herr Wallenberg liked them. I'm really just a beginner."

"Your pictures were excellent," Wallenberg said. "You and Tom will be a real asset to our operation." He glanced at the windshield with a worried look. "This weather isn't going to help these poor Jews, is it? As if they don't already have enough to worry about."

Twenty-five kilometers west of the city the Studebaker overtook the columns of marching Jews who had left Bekasmegyer that morning. The headlights of Wallenberg's car showed barefoot children, women carrying infants and children, and old men dragging their wives. As Vilmos slowed to avoid hitting them, some of the marchers recognized Wallenberg and shouted for help.

Wallenberg slumped in the rear seat and pulled his hat low over his face to conceal his tears. He knew that these Jews, as pathetic as they were, were well off when compared with those who had been on the road for eight days. He was hoping to reach Hegyeshalom in time to rescue some of the Jews who were about to be handed over to Eichmann. If he drove all night, he could reach the frontier by dawn, but if he arrived later than nine o'clock, another three thousand Jews would be beyond rescue.

"Pull over here," Wallenberg told Vilmos as the Studebaker approached Gonyu, one of the designated "rest stops" for the marchers. Several youthful Arrow Cross guards were lounging beside the roadway, so Wallenberg rolled down his window to talk with them. "Do you know where the Jews are being quartered tonight?" he called. "The ones marching to Hegyeshalom?"

One of the Arrow Cross boys was attempting to light a cigarette, but the wind was making the task difficult. In disgust the youth hurled the cigarette against the side of Wallenberg's car. "What does it matter," he growled indifferently. "Who cares about the filthy Jews?"

"They're over there," one of his companions said, pointing in the direction of two abandoned barns. "Can't you smell them?" The other troopers laughed.

Vilmos steered the Studebaker down a narrow, rutted lane toward the barns. As Wallenberg stepped from the car, he pulled a long, silver flashlight from under the seat and switched it on. "No pictures here," he told Tom, who was reaching for his camera. "The flash will make the guards nervous. Wait till morning light."

Hans, Vilmos, and Tom followed Wallenberg toward the barn. Two Arrow Cross troopers stopped them at the door. "You're not allowed in here," one of them barked. "You're trespassing."

Wallenberg handed his flashlight to Vilmos and then opened the long pasteboard box he carried under his arm. He handed a small, flat item to one of the troopers. "Chocolate bars," he said with a flourish. "With almonds."

The troopers' eyes grew wide at the sight of the unusual treat.

"I have forty-eight bars," Wallenberg continued, "and they're yours if you allow me to talk with the Jews inside these barns. How many of you are guarding this rest area?"

"Eight." The trooper who spoke looked longingly at the candy bar in his companion's hand, then at the box in Wallenberg's hands. He couldn't seem to take his eyes off the chocolate.

Wallenberg noticed this and placed a chocolate bar in the young trooper's hands. "Then that's six chocolate bars apiece," he said quietly. "Of course, who's to object if I give you each nine bars and give the others five apiece?"

The young Arrow Cross men greedily stuffed the chocolate bars into their coats as Wallenberg passed the candy to them. The taller youth handed his rifle to his companion and then took the carton of chocolate from Wallenberg's hands, cradling it carefully as if it were a priceless treasure. "Follow us," he said.

As the guards opened the barn doors, the beam of Wallenberg's flashlight swept the interior of the decaying building. Hundreds and hundreds of people lay on filthy piles of straw, groaning and writhing in pain. Some, too exhausted to move, had collapsed in puddles of foul-smelling water. The stench of human waste and unwashed bodies engulfed Hans and the others as they stepped into the barn.

Wallenberg knelt beside a feeble old man who looked as if he were more dead than alive. Vilmos held the flashlight for him. "Have they—" Wallenberg began, but his voice broke with emotion. "Have they fed you today?"

The elderly Jew raised his eyes to stare at Wallenberg. He feebly shook his head.

"Nothing? Nothing at all?"

The man slowly shook his head again.

"Then what about yesterday?" Wallenberg asked gently. He tenderly stroked the old man's face with his right hand as his left hand wiped away his own tears.

"Soup," the old man replied in a weak voice. "One cup of thin soup."

Hans was moved with emotion as he watched Wallenberg and the old man. *Never before have I met such a humble, compassionate man,* he thought. *Lord Jesus,* he prayed silently, *help me learn to demonstrate the same compassion that Wallenberg does.*

Wallenberg patted the old man's shoulder. "We'll be right back," he whispered.

Hans helped Wallenberg, Vilmos, Tom, and the drivers of the trucks as they unloaded sacks of food and dragged them into the barns. The doctors and nurses from the second car scurried back and forth between the two barns as they administered medicine and help to as many suffering Jews as possible. Finally, Wallenberg called them all from the barns. "We have to move on," he said in a husky voice. "There are others who need us even more desperately."

All eight Arrow Cross guards gathered around the Studebaker as the trucks turned around in the barnyard. Wallenberg pulled a roll of bank notes from his coat and passed two to each guard. "Please be sure that each person gets some food," he urged. "Help the ones who are too weak to get it themselves."

The Studebaker rolled back to the roadway. The truck headlights illuminated the car's interior and Hans saw that Wallenberg and the other two men all had tears in their eyes.

Vilmos drove on in the darkness past vineyards and farms and villages toward Hegyeshalom. During the night the car passed the other rest stops—the open mines, the cattle corrals, the open fields. Hans watched the freezing rain pelt the windshield and prayed for the suffering Jews who were spending the long night outside in the bitter weather.

The car lurched over a rough spot in the road, and Hans awoke with a start. A rosy glow brightened the eastern sky behind the car. The long night was nearly over.

"We're nearly at Hegyeshalom," Wallenberg said quietly, as Vilmos guided the Studebaker around a group of marching Jews. "Most of the marchers we're passing are young boys and girls. The older Jews have disappeared."

The caravan arrived at 7:00 a.m., just as the Arrow Cross troops were delivering a collection of Jews to Eichmann's SS at the railway station. The prisoners were in the worst imaginable condition. The hardships of the foot march, the lack of food, the freezing weather, and the fearful realization that they were facing death had brought the pitiful marchers to such a state that all human dignity had left them. They had long ago given up all hope.

The Arrow Cross had divided the Jews into groups of a hundred each. Some of the groups had already been loaded onto freight cars, and the doors were locked and sealed. Other groups of Jews stood on the loading platform, awaiting orders to board.

Wallenberg sprang from the car and showed his diplomatic credentials to the Arrow Cross guards at the entrance to the station. "You are holding Jews with Swedish *Schützpasses!*" he thundered. "Stand aside and let us take the Jews that have passes."

The guards responded by lowering their bayonets against Wallenberg's chest and forcing him away from the station. Vilmos, standing close to the Studebaker, shook his head. "It doesn't look good," he muttered.

Hans noticed that Tom was still in the front seat of the automobile, snapping picture after picture of the heartrending scene on the platform. Hans jumped into the back seat, grabbed the camera that Wallenberg had given him, and went to work.

Wallenberg ran around to the other side of the station, climbed up on the roof of one of the locked freight cars, and shouted through the air vents, "Are there any Jews who have lost their Swedish protective passes?"

Voices inside shouted, "Yes!" Hands shot through the air vents. Wallenberg ran along the roof shoving blank passes into each waiting hand.

One of the Arrow Cross guards noticed Wallenberg's daring rescue attempt and pointed him out to the others. Several guards hurried toward the train. "Hey, you," one of them thundered, "get down from there!"

Wallenberg ignored them and continued passing out the *Schützpasses*. He leaped across to the next freight car and shouted down through the air vents. When hands appeared, he passed out his *Schützpasses* as rapidly as he could.

Several Arrow Cross guards threw their rifles into firing position. Hans's heart seemed to leap into his throat. "No!" he wanted to scream. "Don't shoot him!"

A volley of shots rang out, and Hans winced. But to his astonishment, Wallenberg's body didn't tumble from the roof of the freight car to land upon the platform. The Arrow Cross had deliberately fired over his head.

Wallenberg scrambled down from the roof of the railroad car and disappeared around the corner of the depot. Moments later he appeared at the rear of the Studebaker. He unlocked the trunk, lifted out two small wooden crates, and disappeared again.

"What's he doing?" Hans asked Vilmos, who by now was back inside the car.

The driver shook his head. "With him, I'm never quite sure," he answered. "But he's up to something."

Moments later, Wallenberg returned to the station with a Gendarme officer and a squad of Hungarian soldiers. Intimidated by his show of force, the Arrow Cross guards agreed to allow him to remove any Jews with *Schützpasses* from the train.

Wallenberg turned toward the Studebaker. "Vilmos!" he called. "Tom! Hans! Bring my ledger book and the passes."

Hans hurried onto the loading platform with the others. Wallenberg opened the huge, leather-bound book and called in a loud voice, "I have passes for the following people." He then proceeded to call out a list of the most common Jewish surnames.

Dozens of Jews stepped forward—some having heard their names and others simply daring to hope that this brave man just might rescue them. When they stepped forward, Wallenberg asked them to repeat their full names. Vilmos, Tom, and Hans quickly wrote each name on a blank pass.

The drivers from the three trucks unloaded most of the rest of the food on to the platform and then started leading the rescued Jews toward the trucks. When the trucks were full, Wallenberg turned sadly to the Jews who still waited in line. "I'm sorry," he said, dropping his head, "but I cannot take any more. I'm so sorry."

Hans would never forget the looks of despair on the faces of those who were left behind.

As Wallenberg hurried toward the Studebaker, he spotted the Hungarian military commander of Hegyeshalom. He hurried over to the man and pulled a large roll of bank notes from his coat. Thrusting the money into the commander's hand, Wallenberg said, "Please distribute my food to the Jews who are left behind. At least they can satisfy their hunger once before they leave Hungary."

The trucks rolled from the station, and Wallenberg jumped into the back seat of the Studebaker. Vilmos stepped on the accelerator to catch up to the trucks.

"Three hundred," Wallenberg said quietly. "We rescued just about three hundred." He swallowed hard. "But there were nearly three thousand left behind." He pulled his hat low over his eyes and slumped against the door.

The convoy motored back toward Budapest with the precious cargo of Jewish lives. Every twenty miles or so, they encountered the columns of marching Jews, and Wallenberg insisted on stopping. He and his assistants passed out food and *Schützpasses* while the doctors and nurses dispensed medicine to the worst of the sufferers. Wallenberg passed out bottles of rum to the guards as payment for tolerating his interference.

"So that's how you got the Gendarmes and the soldiers to help you at Hegyeshalom," Hans guessed during one of the stops. "You bribed them with rum."

Wallenberg nodded. "Rum is one of the worst evils on earth," he replied, "but if I can give it to my enemies so that they will release the Jews, then I will."

Several dozen Jews rushed toward the convoy just then, hoping for a place on one of the trucks. Wallenberg met them with tearful apologies. "My trucks are full," he told them sadly. "I can't take any more. I wish I could, but I just can't take any more."

Wallenberg was in agony as he got back into the Studebaker. "These people are all going to die," he told Hans. "Even if their guards would release them, most of them would never make it back to Budapest alive. They're all going to die."

The diplomat was silent for the rest of the trip, sitting slumped against the door with his hat pulled low over his face. As the convoy neared the city, he suddenly stirred and leaned forward eagerly. "Let the trucks continue on to the safe houses," he told Vilmos. "The rest of us will attempt to pull off our most daring rescue yet."

Wallenberg looked from Vilmos to Tom to Hans. "If you three are willing, we'll attempt to rescue the Jews at the Bekasmegyer brickyard. But I'll warn you—this one may get us all killed. To pull off the rescue that I have in mind, we'll be placing ourselves in extreme danger."

"We're with you," Vilmos said quietly.

CHAPTER THIRTEEN

JOZSEFVAROSI STATION AGAIN

Wallenberg's Studebaker rolled toward the center of Budapest, driven by one of the nurses that had participated in the rescues of the night before. The second automobile from the convoy drove in the opposite direction, toward the Bekasmegyer brickyard. Packed inside were Wallenberg, Vilmos, Tom Veres, Hans, three doctors, and a nurse. All were wearing SS uniforms that had come from the trunk of Wallenberg's Studebaker.

"It will be risky," Wallenberg said again, "but I think it will work. Simply follow my lead, but don't speak any more than is necessary. And remember, be just a bit rough with the Jews so it will look good for the Arrow Cross."

He paused. "Our lives are in God's hands. The weapons I gave you are basically worthless. They're not even loaded."

Vilmos wheeled the auto through the gates of the Bekasmegyer brickyard and braked to a stop. Wallenberg quickly scanned the crowded brickyard. "The guards are all Arrow Cross," he said quietly. "That's in our favor. Well, let's do it."

Wallenberg sprang from the car, and the others followed. Hans swallowed nervously. If the Arrow Cross guards saw through the charade, they would all be gunned down instantly. *Lord, watch over us*, he prayed.

Wallenberg strode briskly and confidently toward an Arrow Cross officer. "Are you in command here?"

The Arrow Cross man saluted. "Yes, sir, I am."

Wallenberg returned the salute. "Have your men line up one thousand of these wretched Jew dogs. I want the columns ten abreast. My men will take them from there."

The Arrow Cross officer frowned. "On whose orders?"

Wallenberg flew into a rage. "Are you questioning the authority of an SS officer?"

The Arrow Cross officer nervously eyed the colonel's insignia on Wallenberg's uniform. "No, sir!"

"Then do as you are ordered," Wallenberg thundered. "I want those filthy Jews ready to march out the gates in ten minutes. One thousand of them. Now move! *Mach schnell!*"

Thoroughly intimidated by Wallenberg's authority and fluent German, the officer hurriedly began to issue orders to his men. As Hans watched in astonishment, the Arrow Cross guards lined up their Jewish prisoners in columns at the front gate of the brickyard. The Jews cowered in fear, unaware that the stern Nazi "colonel" was actually their friend and benefactor.

"Move them out!" Wallenberg ordered in a commanding voice when the last of the thousand had taken their place in the waiting columns.

Vilmos and Tom began shouting at the Jews in the front of the columns. "March, you dirty Jews! Move! Can you march on your own, or do we have to persuade you? Move!" They struck out at the marchers with the stocks of their automatic weapons, but Hans noticed that they were not swinging too energetically. The Arrow Cross guards were watching closely.

Hans stepped up behind a Jewish youth about his own age. "Move faster, you dirty Jew!" he shouted, kicking the boy in the seat of the pants. He struck a stout woman across the back with the butt of his rifle, being careful not to swing too hard, but trying to make it look good for the Arrow Cross.

As the last of the throng of hapless Jews moved through the gates, the doctors and nurse brought up the rear, driving the Jews forward with shouts and kicks. Wallenberg saluted the Arrow Cross officer in charge and then got into his automobile and drove away.

Hans watched the faces of the Jews as they stumbled along the muddy roadway. Hopelessness and despair were written on their faces, and he longed to tell them that they were being rescued, not marched to their deaths. *Just wait till you find out who we really are,* he thought gleefully.

A young mother was carrying a little girl who sobbed in fear. Hans reached out and gently stroked the little girl's face, and the mother looked up at him in surprise and alarm. Remembering the importance of maintaining the charade, Hans gave the mother a stern look and stepped away quickly.

Wallenberg's automobile was waiting at the side of the road just over two kilometers from the brickyard. As the columns of marching Jews approached, Wallenberg stepped from the car. Tom and Vilmos called a halt, and the columns came to a standstill.

Wallenberg stepped to the middle of the roadway. The Jews watched him nervously.

Without saying a word, Wallenberg removed his officer's hat and handed it to Vilmos. He slipped out of the stiff colonel's coat and draped it over his arm. "You are not being marched to Hegyeshalom," he shouted. "I am Wallenberg, and you are being rescued!"

Despair turned to sheer joy. "It's Wallenberg!" some of the Jews cried, hugging each other in ecstasy. Others ran forward to hug their deliverer as the marvelous news passed down the lines toward those in the back. Tears of joy streamed down countless faces. Others knelt in the mud to give thanks for their deliverance.

Hans found the boy he had kicked. "I'm sorry," he said sheepishly. "It had to look good for the guards."

The Jewish boy grinned at him. "I don't think I even felt it," he replied.

Hans felt a hand on his shoulder and turned to see the woman he had struck with his rifle. "May God in heaven bless you," the woman beamed. "You're a good lad."

Wallenberg raised his hand for silence, and the exuberant Jews finally became quiet. "We have to continue the march," he shouted, "but you are going to Budapest, not to Hegyeshalom. My assistants will take you to yellow star houses on Ulloi Street. I will go on ahead and alert the other residents that you are coming."

He raised his hand again. "Shalom, my friends. Shalom." As Wallenberg walked to his car, the cheers of the grateful Jews rang in his ears.

Tom Veres and Vilmos started the columns moving again. Hans threw his automatic rifle into the tall weeds at the side of the road. He walked back until he found the tired young mother with the little girl and held out his arms. "How about if I carry her for a while," he offered. "It looks like she's getting heavy."

Wallenberg made several more trips to Hegyeshalom in the next few days, rescuing more than two thousand Jews who were scheduled to die in the death camps at Strasshoff, Austria, and Auschwitz, Poland. Vilmos Langfelder drove and Tom Veres took scores of photographs, but Wallenberg insisted that Hans stay home to help Gretchen and Miklös in their work as couriers.

The Russian armies relentlessly advanced toward Budapest, pushing the Nazis back farther and farther each day. The Arrow Cross became even more desperate, and their reign of terror increased in ferocity. The streets of Budapest were unsafe for anyone, whether Jew or Gentile. Food supplies ran low. Hans, Gretchen, and Miklös spent most of their time delivering food from Wallenberg's caches to starving Jews, but they didn't venture out on the streets. Miklös taught them to travel across the city underground, entering the city cisterns, sewers, and storm drains through trapdoors in basements or manholes in secluded alleys. They carried flashlights with them at all times, and Miklös somehow kept them supplied with fresh batteries.

The call came to Wallenberg's Ulloi Street office one afternoon as the diplomat was giving delivery assignments. "They've gathered all the protected workers and marched them to the Jozsefvarosi freight station," the voice whispered over the telephone. "They're loading them into boxcars for Auschwitz. Please hurry."

Until now the Swedish-protected labor brigades had been spared the horrors of the death march. The seventeen thousand Jewish men on the brigades had been allowed to remain in Budapest, digging trenches and clearing away rubble from the bombing raids. They were the only large group of able-bodied Jews left alive in the capital.

Eichmann had decided to take them. The Hungarian Ministry of the Interior had agreed to "loan" these workers to the Germans for the purpose of building earthworks around Vienna. Eichmann had somehow obtained trains to transport the men to Austria.

Wallenberg hung up the phone and turned to an aide. "Send my staff to Jozsefvarosi station with blank passes. Tell them to hurry!"

The diplomat ran for the door. "Hans, come with me. Vilmos is sick, and I don't have time to round up another driver. We'll have to do this one by ourselves."

Hans followed Wallenberg to the alley behind the building. Wallenberg stood staring in astonishment. His parking spot was empty.

"It's the Arrow Cross," Wallenberg fumed. "They've stolen my car again." He turned toward the door. "Come on. Let's see if we can find a couple of bicycles."

Hans was out of breath by the time he and Wallenberg reached the freight station. He leaped off his bike and raced after Wallenberg through the station gates and up onto the loading platform.

Thousands of Jewish men stood waiting on the platform in front of empty freight cars. Some of the cars had already been loaded, locked, and sealed. But, unlike the scene at the Bekasmegyer brickyard, the SS, not the Arrow Cross, were in charge. When Wallenberg appeared on the loading platform, the young SS transport officer in charge of the operation came rushing over. Drawing his revolver, he pointed it at Wallenberg.

Wallenberg was enraged. "How dare you threaten a diplomatic representative of the king of Sweden?" he shouted. "This is an insult to our diplomatic relations!"

Surprised and unnerved by Wallenberg's outburst, the Nazi officer hesitated and then reholstered his gun.

Wallenberg continued shouting. "There are Jews here that are protected by the king of Sweden," he stormed, gesturing toward the waiting prisoners. "Release them at once! How dare you arrest those who are under His Majesty's protection?"

The Nazi hesitated. Intimidated by the force of Wallenberg's protest, he was uncertain as to what to do. The loading was interrupted as the guards stood and watched the confrontation.

"At once!" Wallenberg shouted. "These people are protected! Release them at once, or I'll file a diplomatic protest with your superiors!"

The officer stepped back, and Hans knew that Wallenberg had won.

Wallenberg strode down the platform yelling, "Anyone holding a Swedish *Schützpasse* fall out of line and go to the south end of the platform." Several dozen men quickly formed a line at the designated place. Wallenberg walked down the line of sealed rail cars. "Open them," he ordered the guards. "There may be men inside with *Schützpasses*." The guards complied.

Wallenberg turned and surveyed the line of Jews at the south end of the platform. There were only about fifty men out of the thousands at the station. He glanced at the young SS officer and then shouted across the station, "Are there any men here who have Hungarian documents proving that you once had a *Schützpasse?*"

A thin Jewish man stepped forward and timidly held out a document toward Wallenberg, who glanced at it and shouted, "Yes! Yes! Go get in line with the others! Are there any others?"

As the man pocketed the piece of paper and hurried toward the south end of the platform, Hans was amazed to see that the document was simply the man's driver's license.

"Are there any others with official documents?" Wallenberg shouted again.

Many of the other Jewish men quickly caught on to the ruse. Fishing in their pockets, they produced library cards, tax receipts, ration cards, and vaccination certificates—any paper that looked official. As they presented these documents to Wallenberg, he pretended to examine them, then shouted, "Yes! You are under Swedish protection. Next! Yes, you may go. Next. Yes, you too." Wallenberg was gambling that the young SS officer could not read a word of Magyar, the Hungarian language.

By now Wallenberg's aides had arrived at the station with the blank *Schützpasses*. Hans hurried toward the south end of the platform. He helped fill out the passes and gave them to the grateful men. The men were loaded onto the trucks along with those holding legitimate passes. The trucks rolled back into Budapest with three hundred men aboard.

One cold day late in November Wallenberg assembled a large group of his staff in his Ulloi Street office. Hans, Gretchen, and Miklös were present.

"I'm sure that many of you have noticed the seven-foot wooden fence that the Arrow Cross has erected around the Jewish sector of the city," the diplomat said gravely. "Vajna and Eichmann have ordered all the unprotected Jews into this new ghetto. There are four gates, one at each point of the compass; the Arrow Cross and the police heavily guard these. We estimate that approximately seventy thousand Jews have been packed into this area in the last few days."

Wallenberg paused, and the staff waited expectantly. Tension filled the air.

Wallenberg cleared his throat. "We're sure that Eichmann is planning a pogrom," he continued, "and will attempt to massacre all these Jews at one time. We'll attempt to deal with that situation as soon as we are made aware of Eichmann's plans.

"Our task right now is to keep these Jews alive. The Jewish quarter is sealed off from the rest of the city, and, as you know, the Arrow Cross will do little or nothing to see that the Jews have even a minimal amount of food. Anyone attempting to smuggle food past the guards will immediately forfeit his life."

Wallenberg paused and looked at Miklös. "My friend Miklös tells me that we can smuggle food to our Jewish friends through the system of tunnels and cisterns beneath the city. We'll need a dozen volunteers; but I'll warn you in advance, the Arrow Cross will show no mercy, and our mission will be extremely dangerous."

The diplomat looked around the room. "Do I have any volunteers?"

Hans and Gretchen were the first ones to step forward.

CHAPTER FOURTEEN
THE GHETTO

"Hans, why don't you and Gretchen take the next one?" Miklös said, as he pointed the beam of his flashlight down a dark, narrow culvert to the right. The men pushing the crude wooden cart slowed it to a standstill in the middle of the sewer main. "You'll only have to crawl about twenty meters or so," Miklös told them. "There's a trapdoor that opens into the basement of house number forty-nine."

Hans climbed up into the tunnel, which was less than a meter in diameter. He turned around to face the main corridor. "All right, I'm ready."

One of the men hefted a twenty-kilogram sack of beans from the cart and lifted it into the tunnel. Hans seized the sack and dragged it down the tunnel a meter or two. Miklös turned to Gretchen. "Think you can handle a ten-kilo sack of flour?"

Gretchen nodded. "I think so." She climbed up into the tunnel after Hans.

Miklös passed the heavy sack of flour up to her. "You and Hans can catch up to us in a couple of minutes." Gretchen nodded, and the heavily loaded cart began to roll down the corridor.

Hans switched on his flashlight. He soon discovered that it was difficult work to drag the heavy sack of beans while holding on to the flashlight. After traveling ten or twelve meters, he stopped to rest. He aimed the flashlight in Gretchen's direction. "How are you making it, Gretchen?"

"All right," Gretchen replied. "But I think the bottom side of the sack is getting wet."

"Then we'll have to hurry so it doesn't soak up too much water," Hans replied. He took a deep breath and then began dragging the sack of beans again. Moments later he came to the trapdoor that Miklös had mentioned.

Hans left the sack of beans below the trapdoor and went back to help Gretchen with the flour. As he grasped the flour sack, he discovered that his sister was right. The bottom side of the sack was slimy and wet from the moisture in the culvert. When he reached the trapdoor, he placed the flour on top of the sack of beans.

Hans stood up and pushed open the trapdoor over his head. He found himself in a dark basement room. Nearly twenty people were lying or sitting on the cold cement floor, and they recoiled in alarm when Hans appeared.

"Wallenberg sent us," Hans called in an attempt to still the Jews' fears. "We brought food."

"Tibor," one of the Jews called. A tall, thin man stepped into the room.

"Who are you?" Tibor demanded of Hans.

"I'm Hans Von Edler," Hans replied. "My sister, Gretchen, is with me. Wallenberg sent us with some food. We have twenty kilos of red beans and ten kilos of flour."

The tall Jew beamed. "Bless you, lad."

Hans stooped and lifted the flour sack to Tibor, who passed it to another man. Hans struggled to lift the heavy sack of beans. Tibor reached down into the opening and grasped one end of the sack. Together, they laid it on the floor.

Hans looked around at the sea of curious faces watching him. "How many people are living in this house?" he asked.

Tibor licked his lips. "At last count," he replied, "there were two hundred sixty-seven."

"Two hundred sixty-seven!" Hans repeated.

"We're just thankful to be alive," Tibor said quietly. "Many of the houses have more than three hundred residents at this time." He shook Hans's hand. "We are grateful for the food. Shalom. Go in peace."

"Two hundred sixty-seven," Hans exclaimed as he followed Gretchen back down the narrow culvert. "Thirty kilos of food is not even enough for one day for that many people. Did you see how thin they were? They looked like living skeletons."

"I wish we could have brought them more," Gretchen responded as she crawled through the dark, wet tunnel. "Maybe some oatmeal, or some potatoes."

"I just hope this war ends soon," Hans replied, "or there won't be any Jews left alive in Budapest."

Two men with another cartload of beans and flour met Miklös and his crew at the end of the sewer main. Miklös guided the cart around a corner and stopped under an iron ladder leading up to a manhole. "This will be the most dangerous part of our run," he told the others quietly. "We can't reach this one section of the ghetto by tunnel, so we'll have to go out on the streets."

Miklös climbed the ladder and pushed his shoulder against the manhole cover. Grunting with the effort, he struggled to raise the cover and finally managed to push it to one side. He climbed two more rungs, looked around outside, and then ducked back down the ladder.

"We'll come out in a deserted alley," he told the others, "but we'll have to be careful. Let's get the food up, and then I'll assign a delivery to each of you."

Moments later, the crew knelt in the alley beside the sacks of food. Miklös gave instructions in a quiet voice. "Andre and Phillipe, take a left at the next block and go three blocks to Bor Aros Street. There's a large, green house on the southeast corner. Take your sacks to the back door.

"Samuel, you and Elias follow them, but take your sacks to the house three doors down. We'll meet back here in fifteen minutes. Watch out for the *Nyalis*. Be careful."

The men shouldered their sacks and trudged down the alley. Miklös handed a sack of flour to Gretchen, and then he and Hans each shouldered a heavy sack of beans. Miklös led them to a large house several blocks away.

After delivering their sacks, Hans, Gretchen, and Miklös hurried back toward the alley meeting point. "What if Wallenberg runs out of food?" Gretchen worried. "These poor people will starve to death."

Miklös nodded. "Seventy thousand people," he replied. "We're nearly working ourselves to death, but I feel like we're trying to feed an army from one soup kettle. There's not enough to go around."

Gretchen suddenly froze. *"Nyalis!"* She pointed down the block.

Four Arrow Cross *Nyalis* were strolling down the street toward them, less than two hundred meters away. Spotting the three young people, the *Nyalis* dashed toward them.

"This way!" Miklös cried. With Hans and Gretchen right behind him, he dashed into a narrow space between two buildings. Reaching an alley behind the buildings, Miklös dashed to the left.

Hans, Gretchen, and Miklös ran until their sides ached and their lungs burned. Miklös seemed to know exactly where he was at all times, and he led them on a circuitous route through alleys, down narrow side streets, and across back yards. Finally, he paused for breath in a secluded alley. "I think we gave them the slip," he panted.

At that moment, the four *Nyalis* appeared at the other end of the alley, less than sixty meters away.

"Follow me," Miklös whispered. He turned and leaped to the hood of a bombed-out automobile, and then leaping upward, caught the top of a tall wooden fence with both hands. Swinging his right leg over the top of the fence, he scrambled over and dropped to the ground on the other side.

As the *Nyalis* raced down the alley, Hans vaulted to the hood of the car and then leaped for the fence. "Come on, Gretchen!" he cried. As he scrambled over the fence, Hans saw Gretchen clamber up on the hood of the car.

Hans dropped to his knees in the grass behind the fence. Leaping to his feet, he raced after Miklös. The Jewish boy darted between two houses, plunged through a gate, and dashed across the street to scramble under a thick hedge in front of a bombed-out building. Lungs bursting, Hans scrambled in right behind him and dropped to the ground. He struggled to catch his breath.

Miklös spoke. "Where's Gretchen?"

Alarmed, Hans twisted around to face the street. "She was right behind me! Miklös, we have to go back!"

At that moment, two *Nyalis* came running through the gate across the street. Reaching the sidewalk, they paused to look up and down the street. Hans and Miklös dropped to their bellies and hugged the ground, hoping that the *Nyalis* could not see them.

Moments later, the other two *Nyalis* stepped through the gate. Hans sucked in his breath sharply. They had Gretchen with them!

Hans looked at Miklös. "We have to do something."

Miklös shook his head. "Hans, there's four of them," he whispered urgently. "There's nothing we can do."

"But they have Gretchen!"

"Hans, there's nothing we can do."

"Well, I'm not just going to lie here and let them take her away," Hans whispered fiercely. He crawled forward, but Miklös seized him and tried to drag him back.

"Hans, listen to me," Miklös insisted, whispering right into Hans's ear. "There's nothing you can do. You'll just get yourself killed and maybe Gretchen too. Let's get Wallenberg. He'll know how to get Gretchen back."

Hans slumped to the ground. His heart cried out in anguish as he watched the four Arrow Cross troops lead his little sister away. Just before they reached the corner, they were met by five more *Nyalis* leading four prisoners: Samuel, Elias, Andre, and Phillipe!

Half an hour later, Hans and Miklös burst into Wallenberg's office.

"They've taken Gretchen!" Hans shouted. "They've taken Gretchen!"

Madame Wohl looked up from her desk. "Slow down, Hans. Who's taken Gretchen?"

"The Arrow Cross!" Hans blurted. "We were in the ghetto delivering food, and four *Nyalis* captured Gretchen. Where's Herr Wallenberg? He has to do something."

Madame Wohl jumped to her feet. "He's been up all night, Hans, and now he's sleeping in one of the back rooms. I'll waken him."

"Please hurry," Hans begged as the woman scurried down the hall. "We have to save Gretchen!"

Wallenberg appeared less than a minute later. He was tucking in his shirt as he hurried into the room. "What happened?" he asked, with concern in his voice.

"They took Gretchen!" Hans cried. "Four *Nyalis*. And they have Samuel, Andre, Phillipe, and Elias. Sir, we have to do something!"

Wallenberg flinched as he heard the news. "I'm sorry, Hans," he said quietly. "I've been fearful that something like this would happen." He grabbed the coat that Madame Wohl held out for him. "They've probably taken her to the Bekasmegyer brickyard."

Wallenberg hurriedly put the coat on. "Vilmos!" he shouted.

Vilmos Langfelder rushed into the room. "Sir?"

"Is the new auto ready?" Wallenberg demanded.

"Yes, sir," Vilmos replied.

"Start it up," Wallenberg ordered. "We leave for Bekasmegyer immediately."

The shiny black Packard raced through the streets of Budapest. *Hurry!* Hans cried inwardly. *Dear God, please help us to find Gretchen in time.*

When Wallenberg's automobile reached the brickyard, a stern-faced Arrow Cross officer stopped it at the gate. Vilmos rolled down the driver's side window. "Turn the auto around," the officer ordered. "No one is allowed inside the yard."

From the back seat of the Packard, Hans could see that the brickyard was packed with Jewish prisoners. He scanned the part of the crowd that he could see, looking for the face of his sister.

Wallenberg walked around the side of the car and approached the officer, displaying his diplomatic credentials. "Raoul Wallenberg, Swedish Legation," he said. "We must be allowed inside."

The officer shrugged. "You heard me. No one gets in. No one."

"I demand to be allowed access to the brickyard," Wallenberg insisted, raising his voice. "Some of my staff have been arrested by mistake. We have reason to believe that they were taken here."

The Arrow Cross man lowered his automatic rifle to point it at Wallenberg's chest. Several guards hurried over and did the same. "Wallenberg," the officer snapped, "your little game is not going to work this time. Leave immediately."

"You have some of my staff," Wallenberg protested. "I'm not leaving until you release them! You have no—"

His words were cut short by the loud report of a rifle. One of the guards had fired a warning shot into the ground at Wallenberg's feet.

The officer stepped forward. "Ten seconds, Wallenberg," he warned, "and then we drop you right here."

Wallenberg backed toward the Packard. "I'll be back," he warned, "with orders from General Schmidthuber himself!"

CHAPTER FIFTEEN
THE SEARCH

Hans tossed and turned on his bed, tormented by the haunting memory of Gretchen being marched along by the four *Nyalis. You should have done something,* he told himself, *but you just let them take her. Some brother you are.*

Hot tears dripped onto his pillow as he whispered in the darkness of his room, "God, help us. Help us to find Gretchen. Don't let them hurt her. Lord, forgive me for not stopping them from taking Gretchen, but I didn't know what to do! I just didn't know what to do."

Hans and Gretchen had always been close, and Hans loved his sister dearly. As they were growing up, he had assumed the role of protective big brother, always watching out for her and standing up for her whenever a neighborhood bully threatened her. And now, at the very time Gretchen had needed him most, he had failed her.

"Gretchen, I'm sorry!" he cried aloud. "I'm sorry. I'm sorry. I just didn't know what to do. I'm sorry! Oh, Gretchen, Gretchen, please forgive me!"

Hans suddenly felt a hand on his shoulder and looked up to see the dark silhouette of Papa leaning over him. "Hans," Papa whispered, "don't blame yourself this way. It's not your fault. Miklös said that there was nothing either one of you could have done."

"But we just let them take her," Hans cried out. "We didn't even try to stop them. It *is* my fault."

"What could you have done against four Arrow Cross men?" Papa asked gently. "Hans, you have to quit blaming yourself."

"I should have let her go first when we scrambled over the fence," Hans replied bitterly. "I should have helped her over. That's where they caught her. Because of me."

Papa sat on the edge of the narrow bed. "Gretchen is in God's hands, Hans. We'll have to trust Him to bring her back to us."

Hans sat up. "Papa, I can't trust anymore. God hasn't stopped the Nazis from killing all these thousands of Jews. You and I both know that many Christians have been killed as well. What if God lets them kill Gretchen?"

Papa sighed. "She's in God's hands, son."

"Sure she is," Hans snarled bitterly, "just like Mama was when the Luftwaffe planes strafed Mittersill."

Two-and-a-half years earlier, German planes had strafed the Austrian village of Mittersill in response to a rumor that the residents were forming a resistance unit. Hans's mother had been killed in the attack. At the time, Hans had had no trouble leaving the matter in God's hands and had experienced inner peace throughout the time of tragedy and loss.

"Hans," Papa was saying, "don't be bitter at God. He's our only hope. We need Him now more than we've ever needed Him before."

Hans remained silent.

"You heard what Herr Wallenberg told us," Papa continued. "He's going directly to General Schmidthuber to try to obtain Gretchen's release and the release of the other staff members."

"He said he'd call," Hans retorted. "So why hasn't the phone rung? We've been waiting all evening!"

"Perhaps he's having trouble getting through to the general," Papa suggested. "Sometimes these things take time, you know."

"Gretchen may not have that much time, Papa. What if Wallenberg can't win this time?"

"Our hope is in God, Hans," Papa reminded, "not Wallenberg." He squeezed Hans's shoulder. "Let's kneel right now and pray for Gretchen, shall we? And let's pray for the Jews that are suffering right now, too."

Hans wept as his father cried out to God, asking for protection for Gretchen, and asking that Wallenberg would be successful in getting a special release from the Nazi general. Nearly an hour after Hans crawled back into bed, he drifted into a troubled sleep.

The insistent jangling of the phone jarred him awake. Papa reached it before he did. *"Ja, ja,"* Papa said into the phone as Hans listened anxiously. "*Gut! Ja,* we'll be ready."

Papa was smiling as he hung up the phone. "That was Vilmos Langfelder," he told Hans. "Wallenberg got the release from General Schmidthuber just now. They're coming right away to pick us up and take us to the brickyard."

The ride to the Bekasmegyer brickyard seemed to take forever. There was a brief delay at an Arrow Cross checkpoint, and that made the situation even worse. Finally, the Packard rolled up to the iron gates of the brickyard.

"This doesn't look good," Vilmos said, and Hans leaned forward in alarm. From where he sat, he could see no prisoners. The brickyard appeared to be empty.

Hans leaped from the back seat and dashed toward the gates. Realizing that they were unlocked, he seized one side and flung it open, then ran inside. He stared about him in dismay. Last night, the yard had been filled with prisoners, but now it was empty. The prisoners were gone.

Wallenberg, Papa, and Vilmos appeared at his elbow. "We were too late!" Hans cried out. "They've taken them to the trains."

Wallenberg nodded slowly. "I'm afraid you're right, Hans," he said quietly. "We missed them."

A lone Arrow Cross guard slipped through the gates and approached the distraught group. "May I help you?" he sneered. "Was there a particular prisoner that you were looking for?"

"Where are the prisoners that were here last night?" Wallenberg asked.

"I'm so sorry, sir," the guard mocked, "but you've missed them. They've taken the train to Auschwitz."

"When did they leave?" Wallenberg demanded.

The guard laughed. "You're too late to catch them," he sneered. "They marched out of here nearly two hours ago. The train would have left the station more than thirty minutes ago." He saluted mockingly. "No more questions, sir? Very well, sir." He turned on his heel and strode through the gate.

"Don't give up hope," Wallenberg tried to console Hans. "We don't even know that Gretchen or the other staffers were even here last night. She may not be on that train. We'll do some checking."

Hans walked across the silent brickyard. "If only we could have gotten her out last night."

Papa caught up with him. "You heard what Wallenberg said, son. We don't know for sure that Gretchen was even in this group of prisoners. If she wasn't, then she's still in the city somewhere. God will help us find her."

A brightly colored piece of cloth lay in the mud at Hans's feet, and his heart seemed to stop as his eye fell upon it. Hans ran forward and picked it up. "Look, Papa!" he exclaimed. "This is Gretchen's scarf! She *is* on the train for Auschwitz."

Papa's hands trembled as he took the cloth from Hans.

The Packard's tires screamed in protest as Vilmos gunned the car around the end of the freight depot and screeched to a stop beside the loading docks. Hans's heart sank. The station was empty. The train was gone.

Wallenberg leaped from the car and ran toward three Arrow Cross youths loitering in front of the depot. Hans saw him reach into his pocket and then hand something to each of the troopers. After a very brief conversation, the diplomat dashed back to the car.

"Take the road to Esztergom!" he shouted at Vilmos. "The train pulled out less than thirty minutes ago! Perhaps we can intercept them before they reach the border."

Vilmos threw the car into reverse and backed from the station. The tires screeched on the pavement as the car leaped forward and shot onto the highway. Vilmos accelerated hard, and the engine roared. Trees and fence posts along the side of the highway dissolved into a blur. Hans glanced over at Papa. His eyes were closed, and Hans knew that he was praying for Gretchen.

"We'll catch them," Vilmos declared. "This Packard has power to spare, and no train is going to outrun it!"

Hope began to build in Hans's heart. Wallenberg would be able to get Gretchen released, once they caught the train. Hans was sure of it.

"Uh-oh," Vilmos muttered. "Trouble."

An Arrow Cross checkpoint loomed ahead. A heavy iron barricade spanned the road, and three *Nyalis* stood beside the road with automatic rifles held at the ready. Vilmos braked hard, and the Packard fishtailed a bit as the tires screamed in protest. The car stopped just five meters from the barricade.

"You're in just a bit of a hurry, aren't you?" an Arrow Cross trooper said as he approached the driver's side of the car. "What's your business?"

Wallenberg leaned forward and held his diplomatic credentials over Vilmos's shoulder. "Swedish Legation," he said, "on official business. Please let us pass."

"Don't be in such a hurry," the *Nyala* admonished. "I need to see your papers, all of you, and you must state your business." He gestured toward Vilmos with the barrel of his rifle. "You first. Papers, please."

Hans sighed, frustrated at the delay. "Lord Jesus, please help," he prayed. "Don't let them delay us so long that we miss the train. Please, Lord Jesus!"

Wallenberg stepped from the car. He hurried to the rear of the car, opened the trunk, and took out three bottles. As he handed the bottles to the trooper, he leaned forward and whispered something to him. The trooper nodded.

"Let them pass," he called to one of his companions, who immediately raised the barricade.

Wallenberg jumped back into the car. "Let's go!" he told Vilmos.

Vilmos pulled away from the checkpoint. He watched his rearview mirror until the car rounded a curve in the road, then accelerated hard. The Packard leaped forward.

After an hour of high-speed travel, Vilmos began to slow down. "The Esztergom station is just ahead," he told the others. "If we've beaten the train, perhaps we can stop it here. But this is our last chance before they cross the border."

The Packard screeched to a stop beside a tiny outpost station. The four occupants leaped out and ran to the depot. An elderly Hungarian met them at the window.

"Did a train pass here within the last half-hour?" Wallenberg asked breathlessly.

The old man shook his head. "Hasn't been a single train yet today."

Wallenberg nodded. "Good. Then we need you to flag down the next train. It's due to pass here at any minute."

The stationmaster looked doubtful. "One of Eichmann's trains?"

Wallenberg nodded. "Yes."

The old man shook his head. "Can't do it. The Nazis would kill me for stopping a train without the proper authorization."

Wallenberg whipped a folded document from his coat and spread it on the counter. "From General Schmidthuber himself," he stated. "The general has granted a special release to four Jews and a Gentile girl on that train. Now, please flag it for us."

The stationmaster pursed his lips as he studied the paper. "Looks official enough. But it still goes against regulations. How come they didn't notify me on the wire?"

Wallenberg was exasperated. "Sir, the train will be along at any minute. If we miss it, five innocent people will go to Auschwitz. Would you want that on your conscience?"

The old man shook his head. "No, I don't think so. Better flag that train, huh?" He reached for a lever at the side of the window. "This will set up a red light, alerting the engineer to stop. And I'll use the flags as well, just to be sure."

He reached under the counter and pulled out a faded red flag, then handed it to Hans. "Run up the track a ways, would you, son? Five hundred meters from here you'll see a bridge that spans a little creek. Post this flag on the signal just beyond the bridge."

Hans grabbed the flag and ran down the tracks. He posted the flag on top of the signal and then dashed back. Just as he reached the depot, he heard the whistle of the train. The train chugged to a stop beside the depot, and an angry SS transport officer leaped off and strode across the platform. "What's the meaning of this?" he berated the elderly stationmaster.

Wallenberg met him and handed him the document from General Schmidthuber. "Wallenberg, Swedish Legation," he said politely. "We're sorry for the delay, but there are five prisoners aboard that were arrested by mistake. They all have valid *Schützpasses,* I assure you."

The officer looked Wallenberg up and down. "I ought to shoot you on the spot," he raged.

Wallenberg placed a roll of bills in the man's hand. "I trust that this will make up for any inconvenience I have caused."

The officer glanced at the money and thrust it in his pocket. "Five minutes," he barked. "If you don't find your people in five minutes, the train rolls with them onboard."

Wallenberg was already running for the train. "Open the cars," he ordered the SS guards who by now were standing on the platform. "Start with the first car."

Moments later, as the guards opened the second car, Philippe sprang onto the platform. "Wallenberg!"

Wallenberg hurried over. "Are the others with you?"

Just then the three other staff members managed to squeeze their way out of the car. "Are we glad to see you!" they chorused.

"What about Gretchen?" Wallenberg asked quickly. "Was she aboard this train?"

One of the men nodded. "We tried to stay together, but she got separated from us. She must be in one of the last cars."

Hans ran toward the rear of the train. "Gretchen," he shouted. "Gretchen Von Edler! Answer me, Gretchen!" As he passed each car, he shouted her name again, and then paused and listened for a reply.

Wallenberg spun around and grabbed an SS guard. "Quickly," he urged. "Get the other cars open."

Only three cars remained to be searched when the transport officer approached Wallenberg. "Your time is up," he said flatly. "This train must roll."

"Two more minutes," Wallenberg argued. "We only have to search the last three cars."

"*Nein*. Your time is up." The officer spun on his heel and barked, "All aboard! Seal the cars and board. This train leaves in thirty seconds."

Hans grabbed Wallenberg by the arm. "Don't let them leave," he begged. "Gretchen is in one of those cars. Please, don't let them leave!"

Wallenberg dashed to the Packard and threw open the trunk. He seized a wooden crate of rum and ran back to the loading platform with it. "Two more minutes," he begged, handing the officer one of the bottles. "Allow us to check the last three cars, and the entire case is yours as payment for the inconvenience."

The officer slid the bottle of rum back into its place and then picked up the whole crate. "*Danke schön*," he said mockingly, "I do appreciate the gift. But this train will not be delayed further." Carrying the case of rum, he strode quickly across the platform and boarded the train.

"Nein!" Hans screamed as the train began to roll from the station. "You can't leave! My sister is on this train!"

Hans ran to Wallenberg and fell to his knees. "You can stop the train. Please, make them stop! Gretchen is still on it. Don't let them take her to Auschwitz."

Wallenberg covered his face with his hands.

Hans leaped to his feet and ran to the edge of the platform. Leaning out, he grabbed the door handle of one of the passing freight cars. He ran along the platform holding onto the handle, trying to pull backwards against the momentum of the train. "Stop the train!" he screamed. "Stop the train!" In his grief, Hans failed to realize the futility of his actions. He was desperately trying to save his sister.

Papa ran forward and pulled his hands from the door handle. "You can't stop the train, Hans! You'll be killed!" He pulled Hans away from the edge of the platform. The boy sank to his knees sobbing.

Wallenberg came over and knelt beside him. Tears streamed down the man's face as he wrapped his arms around Hans. "There's nothing more we can do, Hans," he wept. "We did our best, but there's nothing more we can do for Gretchen."

CHAPTER SIXTEEN
AUSCHWITZ

Gretchen had managed to scramble to the hood of the car in the alley. Leaping upward, she grabbed the top rail of the fence and pulled herself to the top. At that moment, she felt a strong hand grip her ankle.

"You're not going anywhere, girl," a harsh voice called. The Arrow Cross trooper jerked hard on her ankle, and Gretchen fell from the fence to land at the man's feet. He grabbed one of her braids and pulled her to her feet. "Come on, you're going with us."

Gretchen's heart pounded with fear as she followed the two troopers, dragged along by one of her braids. The Arrow Cross had captured her! What would happen now? Where was Hans? Had he and Miklös been captured, too, or would they be able to get word to Wallenberg?

The *Nyalis* took Gretchen through a gate and out onto a street to join the other two troopers. Gretchen looked around but saw no sign of Hans or Miklös. Apparently, they had gotten away.

She heard a voice call out in Magyar. As she looked in the direction of the sound, her heart sank. Coming down the street toward them were five more Arrow Cross *Nyalis*, and they were leading the four Jewish men from Wallenberg's staff!

"So you caught one, too?" one of the *Nyalis* said, eyeing Gretchen. He reached out a dirty hand and jerked Gretchen's hat from her head. "Hey, she's not a Jew. She's Aryan!"

"No, but she was helping the Jews!" one of her captors replied. "She and two boys were delivering food to the Jew dogs."

"Where are they?" The question came from a tall, skinny youth with pimples on his face.

"They got away," a *Nyala* answered, "but we got this one." The *Nyala* stepped toward Gretchen. Placing the barrel of his rifle under Gretchen's chin, he forced her to raise her face toward him. "Hey, you're awfully cute!"

Cold fear tightened around Gretchen's chest, and a chill of horror went up her spine.

"Well, let's take them in," another Arrow Cross man suggested. "It's too cold to stand out here talking."

"Wait," the skinny youth said. "If we take them into headquarters, Captain Lapid will take the credit for the capture. Why don't we take them directly to the brickyard?"

"Or to the river," another suggested. Gretchen knew all too well the fate of prisoners who were marched to the river. She began to pray.

"The brickyard's closer," the skinny one argued. "I say we take them there."

"Kasser's right," another trooper said. "Let's just dump them at the brickyard."

After a cold, long march, the Arrow Cross troopers and their five captives reached the Bekasmegyer brickyard. A guard opened the gate as they approached. The *Nyalis* marched the four men inside but when Gretchen started to enter, one of the younger troopers held her back. "Wait, sweetheart, I haven't had a kiss."

Horrified, Gretchen twisted free of his grasp and dashed inside the brickyard. Her heart was still pounding as she dropped to the cold ground beside Andre and Samuel.

A biting wind swept through the brickyard, and Gretchen shivered. She was thankful that Hans had insisted that she wear her heaviest coat, even though they were planning to work in the relative warmth of the cisterns and culverts under the city. Remembering her birthday scarf, she pulled it from beneath her coat and tied it around her face. The bright colors would not matter now.

"Don't be afraid, Gretchen," Samuel whispered, leaning over to her. "Once Wallenberg knows we're here, he'll have us out in no time. He's already rescued me more than once."

Gretchen nodded and leaned against him for warmth. "I hope so," she said.

A short while later, a shiny black Packard with a blue and yellow flag on each side of the hood pulled up to the iron gates. Andre pointed. "Look. Here's Wallenberg to get us out."

The men raised up on their knees in their eagerness, and Gretchen found herself doing the same. She saw one of the Arrow Cross guards walk toward Wallenberg's Packard and point his weapon at the driver's window. Moments later, Wallenberg himself appeared from around the fender of the car. He was shouting and gesturing wildly. Gretchen saw an Arrow Cross officer stride forward and point a rifle at Wallenberg's chest, and then, seconds later, several other *Nyalis* did the same.

"They're going to shoot him," she groaned.

Samuel laughed. "It's Wallenberg," he said. "They won't dare. Don't worry, he'll get us out."

Just then, a shot was fired, and Gretchen looked up in alarm. Wallenberg was backing hurriedly toward his car. As Gretchen and the four Jewish men watched in disbelief, the Packard backed away from the gates and sped away.

Samuel frowned. "That's the first time I've ever seen the Arrow Cross back Wallenberg down." A worried look replaced his usual cheerful grin.

The morning sun dawned huge and red over the eastern walls of the Bekasmegyer brickyard. Gretchen stirred and thrust her hands inside her coat in an effort to warm her frozen fingers. The night had been so long and so cold. "Dear God," she prayed, "please help Herr Wallenberg to get us out. And help Hans and Papa not to worry about me. Let them know that I'm all right."

A barrage of gunfire from an automatic weapon caused her to jump in fright. She looked up to see an Arrow Cross man standing atop a loading dock. "Jew dogs, stand to your feet!" the man bellowed through a bullhorn. "We're taking you for a little train ride. Free tickets to Auschwitz for everyone, courtesy of Berlin. Stand to your feet!" Arrow Cross troops swarmed across the brickyard, cursing and beating any unfortunate prisoner that was unable to get to a standing position in time. Gretchen winced as she watched an Arrow Cross woman beat a young mother in front of her two small children. The vast throng of Jews shuffled fearfully toward the gates.

After a forced march that seemed like hours, the columns of marching Jews reached the rail station. Gretchen stared apprehensively at the waiting train. "Lord Jesus, let Wallenberg hurry," she prayed quietly. "Please, let Wallenberg hurry!"

The cursing guards drove the crowd onto the loading platform and began to divide the Jews into groups of one hundred each. "Stay close to us," Samuel whispered. Gretchen clung to his arm.

A huge Arrow Cross woman stepped forward and seized Gretchen's arm. "Let go of him and come with me," she ordered.

Gretchen was terrified. "But I'm with them," she whimpered.

The Arrow Cross woman laughed. "I noticed, sweetness," she taunted. "That's why I want you to come with me." She drew a pistol and pointed it at Samuel. "Now come with me, or I shoot him right here."

Overcome with horror, Gretchen allowed herself to be led toward the rear of the train. The woman deliberately placed her in a group that was boarding the last car. When Gretchen's turn came, she hesitated at the edge of the platform. A hard blow across the back knocked her into the freight car.

Gretchen found herself standing in a crowd of sobbing Jews, mostly women. They were packed in so tightly that she could barely move. When the freight car was loaded so full that there was not room for another person, a guard placed a bucket of water between the feet of the woman closest to the door. Another guard tossed a single loaf of bread into the car, and the door slammed closed. Gretchen heard the ominous sound of the door being locked.

A shriek of anger echoed across the freight car, and Gretchen turned to see several people engaged in a vicious struggle. The loaf of bread had landed near the middle of the car, and the prisoners were fighting to get a piece. Gretchen turned away in sorrow. These poor, desperate people were acting like animals.

The women around her slowly sank to their knees, and Gretchen joined them. There was no room to sit comfortably, much less lie down. Gretchen found herself pushed against a thin woman with a little baby. The infant was crying, but the mother made no effort to comfort or quiet it. Gretchen looked into the woman's face. The woman was staring straight ahead, her eyes glazed and expressionless. Gretchen reached out and stroked the baby's head, and the crying subsided.

The freight car swayed as the train rolled from the station. Gretchen felt something drip onto her hand and looked down. The back of her dirty hand was spattered with tears; she realized that she was crying.

The train slowed to a stop sometime later. Gretchen heard shouting. There were no windows in the freight car, but a small amount of light came through the crack over the door. Gretchen wondered what was happening and wished that she could see. The commotion outside the train continued.

Suddenly, she heard Hans's voice calling her name. "Hans!" she screamed. "I'm in here! I'm in the last car!" She paused and listened.

"Gretchen!" the voice called again. "Gretchen, where are you?" Gretchen's heart leaped. It was definitely Hans's voice. He had found her!

"Hans!" she shouted, struggling to rise to her feet. "Hans, I'm here! I'm in the last car!" Gretchen tried to push her way to the door of the cattle car, but the people around her were packed in too tightly. She just couldn't squeeze through.

"Hans!" she wailed. "Please help me! I'm in the last car!" At that moment, she heard the wail of the train whistle, and the car lurched forward as the train began to move. "Hans!" she screamed. "Please help me!"

The car swayed from side to side, and the wheels clicked against the rails as the train picked up speed. Gretchen sank to the floor of the car in defeat. "Lord, Jesus," she prayed, "please help me."

The bar of light at the top of the door had disappeared, and Gretchen knew that night had fallen. She shivered with the bone-numbing coldness that had crept into the freight car. Gretchen ached all over. She drew her hands deeper inside her coat sleeves and sat on the ends of the sleeves in an effort to seal out the cold.

She was so hungry, so cold, and so thirsty! The freight car swayed sharply as the train rounded a tight curve, and Gretchen could tell that they were traveling through steep mountains. Her thoughts went to Hans, and then to Papa. "Dear Lord Jesus," she whispered, "will I ever see them again?"

Gretchen turned and gazed to her left, but it was too dark to see anything. She thought of the thin mother with the little baby. Neither of them had made a sound for almost three days, and she wondered why. An overwhelming sadness engulfed her as the answer came to her.

The metallic screech of brakes broke through her troubled thoughts, and she realized that the train was slowing down. The car lurched forward and then came to a standstill. Gretchen sat in the cold darkness, waiting. What was happening? She heard voices.

The door to the freight car slid open, and a pale yellow light streamed into the darkness of the car. Three Nazi soldiers stood in the doorway, appearing to Gretchen as dark silhouettes. "On your feet, Jew dogs," one of them barked. "Move. Move! *Schnell machen!*" The prisoners closest to the door struggled to their feet and limped from the car.

The soldiers switched on flashlights and moved into the car. They dragged the bodies of those who had died or were too weak to stand to one end of the car. Cursing and shoving, they drove the others from the car. Terror overwhelmed Gretchen as she moved toward the door.

"Why are we in such a hurry?" one soldier asked.

"Eichmann's orders," another Nazi replied. "He wants this load gone before morning."

Gretchen reached the door of the cattle car. She saw a long line of prisoners stretching into the darkness ahead. A short distance from the train, floodlights lit up the two huge buildings into which the captives were marching.

Fear stabbed at her heart. This was Auschwitz.

CHAPTER SEVENTEEN
HANS'S DECISION

"Hans, watch out!" Miklös cried, leaping forward to shove Hans off the sidewalk. The wall of a nearby building collapsed in a crumbling barrage of falling bricks, and the huge glass and steel cafe sign crashed down to the sidewalk in the very spot where Hans had been standing just moments before.

Hans and Miklös dashed to safety across the street. They stood side by side in a doorway, watching as the building before them disintegrated into a tangled heap of rubble. "Thanks, Miklös," Hans breathed, "that was close. If you hadn't pushed me out of the way, that sign would have flattened me for sure!"

Miklös grinned. "Glad to do it. Flat friends aren't much fun."

Hans glanced skyward. "You know, I didn't even hear the planes."

Miklös shook his head. "That wasn't a bomb, Hans. It was a Russian artillery shell."

Hans was surprised. "Are the Russians that close?"

The Jewish boy nodded. "They've broken through the Nazi defenses to the north of the city. They'll be taking Budapest within a week or two. So now we not only have the threat of the bombers, we also have the constant danger of artillery shells."

Miklös checked the street and then slipped cautiously from the doorway. "Let's get out of here." Hans hurried to catch up with him.

Miklös led the way to a nearby storm drain. He pulled a flashlight from his pocket and switched it on as Hans slipped past him into the opening. "What's on your mind, Hans?" Miklös asked. "Just before the shell hit, you seemed to be in another world."

Hans shrugged.

"You were thinking about Gretchen, weren't you?" Miklös asked gently.

Hans stopped and turned to face his friend in the darkness of the tunnel. "It's been three weeks, Miklös, but the pain is just as great as it was the day they took her. Gretchen and I were very close." He tried to choke back a sob. "I kept hoping and praying that somehow Wallenberg or God would get her free. But you heard what Wallenberg told us. Eichmann had all the prisoners at Auschwitz taken to . . . to the . . ." Hans stopped, sobbing so hard he could not continue. "She's gone, Miklös. Gretchen . . ."

Miklös squeezed Hans's shoulder. "I'm sorry, Hans." He hung his head. "I miss her, too."

Hans nodded sadly. "Life will never be the same without Gretchen." He sighed deeply and wiped his eyes. "Let's hurry home."

Papa looked up from his Bible as Hans entered the apartment. "*Guten tag*, son. How was your day?"

Hans stepped to the window and looked out over the quiet street below. "*Gut,* Papa," he mumbled.

"What did you and Miklös do today?" Papa asked, trying to make conversation.

Hans shrugged. "We just made food deliveries, Papa. Miklös and I spent the entire day delivering food to Jews who can't seem to provide for themselves."

Papa glanced up in surprise. "Hans, you seem resentful toward the Jews; that surprises me. They're not leeches. They're a people who have been persecuted and oppressed by men and women filled with hatred."

Hans turned from the window. "Gretchen would still be alive if it weren't for the Jews," he said angrily. "We were delivering food when she was captured." Tears filled his eyes, and he quickly turned back to the window.

Papa slipped up behind Hans and placed a hand on his shoulder, "Gretchen's in heaven, Hans," he said huskily. "She's with Jesus." He cleared his throat. "And she's with Mama." Papa's voice broke, and Hans stole a quick glance at him just in time to see him wipe away a tear.

"I wish we had never come to Hungary."

Papa squeezed Hans's shoulder. "Don't say that, son. Think of how God has used you and Gretchen since you've been here. You've saved the lives of numerous Jews. Think about Herr Szekacs and his children. Think about little Hannah. They would have died if you and Miklös and Gretchen hadn't found them."

Hans turned to face him. "I'm through, Papa," he said quietly. "I-I just can't help Herr Wallenberg anymore. I'm going to ask Miklös to tell him tomorrow."

"But why?"

Hans's lips quivered with emotion. "Because of Gretchen, Papa. Every time we make a delivery I start to hand her a sack of flour or a tin of milk powder, but she's not there. Every time we spot the Arrow Cross *Nyalis,* I turn to make sure that she's seen them. And every time, I remember that she'd still be alive if we hadn't been helping Wallenberg and the Jews."

"So you're blaming Herr Wallenberg for Gretchen's death?"

"*Nein,* Papa," Hans faltered. "I-I guess I'm blaming . . . well, I'm not blaming anybody! But I'm not going to help Wallenberg after today."

Papa nodded. "I see. So you're just going to let the Jews suffer anything the Germans decide to dish out, but you're not going to lift a finger to help?"

Hans exploded in anger. "What about you, Papa? What are you doing to help the Jews? You come by Wallenberg's office from time to time to check on us, but you haven't done anything to save Jewish lives!"

Hans regretted the words the moment they were out. "I'm sorry, Papa," he said immediately. "I didn't mean to be disrespectful."

Papa smiled sadly. "You're forgiven, son." He studied his fingernails for a moment. "I guess I might as well tell you. I've been working for Wallenberg also."

Hans stared at Papa in surprise. "You?"

Papa nodded. "Wallenberg has informants all over the city, helping him keep abreast of what Eichmann and Vajna are doing, and when the Nazis or Arrow Cross are making raids. Many of the informants in our sector of Budapest report to me, and I pass the information on to Wallenberg's office."

Hans looked at his father with new respect. "I didn't know, Papa."

Papa smiled. "The times you saw me at Wallenberg's office, I wasn't checking on you; I was reporting information that couldn't be relayed by telephone, or delivering a document of some sort. I was a go-between to help protect the identity of the informants."

Hans turned back to the window. "I'm glad you're helping, Papa, but I'm through. I can't do it anymore. I keep thinking of Gretchen."

"So you're just going to let Miklös handle your share of the deliveries?"

"Miklös is a Jew," Hans retorted. "He's just helping his own people. I'm not Jewish."

Papa stepped to the window to stand beside Hans. "What about Herr Wallenberg?" he asked softly. "He's not Jewish. Why do you think he left the safety of Sweden, a neutral country, to come to war-torn Budapest? I'll tell you why—because he has a servant's heart, and he has a passion to save the Jewish people, even though they're not his people."

He put his arm around Hans. "Son, you have worked hard and gone through many dangers. I am very grateful for such a brave son and daughter. But now you say you are finished. May I ask, what has happened to your servant's heart?"

Papa's words struck home, and Hans found himself blinking back new tears. "I want to be a servant, Papa; I really do. And I wanted to help the Jews. But I didn't think that Gretchen would die because we were helping. I mean, I knew there was danger and all, but somehow, I just never thought that anything could happen to Gretchen."

Papa wiped his eyes with the back of his fist. "Hans, every time you and Gretchen walked out that door to run a mission with Miklös, my heart cried out to call you back and make you stay in the apartment. I knew you were facing danger. Instead, I had to drop to my knees and commit you to God."

Hans was silent.

"Hans, have you lost your servant's heart?"

Hans dropped his head and studied the windowsill. "*Nein,* Papa," he said, "but I just can't get over losing my sister."

"So you're willing to be a servant," Papa said gently, "as long as it doesn't cost too much."

Hans swallowed hard. "Oh, Papa."

Papa wrapped his arms around Hans. "Hans, I miss Gretchen just as much as you do. These last three weeks I have hurt inside every moment of every day. I miss her voice, her laughter, her sweet smile." His eyes welled up with tears. "But I have to tell myself that she's in heaven with Jesus and that God used her to save some lives and to be a servant to the Jewish people who were suffering so."

He cleared his throat. "The decision is yours, son, and I'll not push you in any way. But if you do decide not to help Herr Wallenberg, I think you need to tell him in person, rather than relaying a message through Miklös."

"But, Papa—"

Papa shook his head. "It's the right way to do it, son. I'll let you do it by telephone, if you wish, to spare you the risk of traveling to his office."

Hans sighed. "I'll go to his office tomorrow."

Hans sat in the hallway across from Madame Wohl's desk. He looked up as the receptionist walked into the room. "He's on the phone, Hans," she said, speaking of Wallenberg, "but he knows you're here. He'll be with you in just a minute."

Hans nodded and swallowed nervously. He wasn't looking forward to telling Wallenberg that he was quitting.

"Hans!" a tiny voice shouted, and Hans turned to see little Hannah Szekacs race across the room toward him. The four-year-old leaped into his lap and wrapped her tiny arms around his neck. "I missed you, Hans."

Hans tousled her curls. "I missed you, too, Hannah." He turned to Madame Wohl. "What is she doing here?"

Madame Wohl smiled. "Her papa is now the baker for a number of Wallenberg's yellow star houses. Wallenberg has Hannah here so the doctor can look at her infected ear."

Hans gave the little girl a hug. "Did her mother pull through?"

Madame Wohl shook her head sadly. "She died the second day she was in the hospital."

Hans sighed heavily.

"But the rest of the Szekacs family is doing just fine," Madame Wohl continued, "thanks to you and Gretchen and Miklös."

Hannah took one of Hans's hands in her lap and began to trace her tiny fingers across the lines in his palm. Hans thought about the day that he, Gretchen, and Miklös had discovered the frightened Szekacs family living under the bushes in Saint Gellert Park.

"Hans, Madame Wohl said that you wanted to see me about something important." Startled, Hans looked up to see Wallenberg standing beside him. "What can I help you with?" the diplomat asked.

Hans glanced at little Hannah Szekacs and then back to Wallenberg. "It . . . it wasn't important, sir. I think I'll find Miklös and help him with the deliveries."

One of Wallenberg's aides entered the room just then. He hurried to Wallenberg's side. "Sir, Eichmann has just ordered the Jewish Council to assemble at the council headquarters at nine o'clock tonight. We have information that he's planning to kill them all."

Wallenberg seemed distressed by the news. "We've been expecting this," he said. "He's planning to kill them so there will be nothing to stand in his way when he massacres the rest of the Jewish population."

He turned to Hans. "Find Miklös as fast as you can," he instructed. "He's the fastest courier we have. I want you two to find every member of the council and warn them to go into hiding. Be careful, but hurry. You must reach them before Eichmann does."

CHAPTER EIGHTEEN

EICHMANN'S LAST MOVE

Christmas was just three days away, but the city of Budapest was not celebrating the gift of God's Son, the one who offers peace and hope. Instead, the city was facing death and destruction, caught between the opposing forces of the German Nazis and the Russian Bolsheviks.

As the Red Army relentlessly pounded the Nazi forces, each day advancing closer to the city, Wallenberg and his courageous staff worked desperately to save as many Jewish lives as possible. They knew all too well that Eichmann intended to kill every last Jew in Budapest before the Nazis were forced to surrender. They also knew that he had a personal interest in killing the members of the Jewish Council.

Hans switched on his flashlight as he slipped into the storm culvert behind Wallenberg's Ulloi Street office. He crawled down the narrow culvert, dropped into the main tunnel, and ran full speed through the darkness. Miklös would probably be making deliveries to the yellow star houses north of Erzsebert Square, and Hans planned to intercept him in the main storm sewer.

Hans came to a huge crack in the floor of the tunnel, the result of a surface hit by a Russian bomb. The stonework on one wall had collapsed. A small pile of stone and mortar lay in the center of the tunnel. Hans leaped over the debris. "Watch out for the junk on the floor," he called instinctively to Gretchen. A cold pain of sorrow tightened in his chest as he remembered that she was no longer with him.

Hans ran until his lungs burned and his sides heaved with pain. Reaching the main tunnel in the vicinity of Erzsebert Square, he sprinted with renewed energy. If he and Miklös failed to warn the members of the Jewish Council, some of them would die.

Finally, when his legs grew weak and shaky and his lungs felt as though they would burst, Hans stopped to catch his breath, leaning over with his hands on his knees. Just as he switched his flashlight off to save the batteries while he rested, a voice called from the darkness. "Hans. Is that you?"

"Miklös," Hans said with a laugh, "you scared me."

"What are you doing here?" Miklös asked. "I thought you went to see Wallenberg."

"Wallenberg wants us to drop everything and find the members of the Jewish Council," Hans said breathlessly. "Eichmann is ordering them to assemble at the council headquarters tonight at nine o'clock, but Wallenberg has learned that it's a trap. Eichmann's going to kill them. We're supposed to warn each of the men to go into hiding immediately."

Miklös let out a low whistle. "If Eichmann is planning to kill the Jewish Council tonight, the rest of us Jews can't be too far behind."

Hans nodded. "We have to hurry."

Miklös thought quickly. "You take the five council members that live on the west end of Pest," he told Hans. "I'll take the others. Here. I'll draw you a map showing you how to find where they are staying."

Nearly an hour later, Hans knocked breathlessly on the door of Samu Stern, the head of the Jewish Council. A young man peered cautiously through a window and then opened the door. "Come in, come in," he urged.

Hans stepped into the narrow foyer. "I need to see Samu Stern," he said. "It's urgent."

An elderly Jewish man appeared in the doorway. "I am Samu Stern."

"Sir, don't go to the council headquarters tonight. It's a trap."

"But Colonel Eichmann has ordered it," the elderly Jew argued. "We must go. It will not bode well for our people if we disobey the colonel's orders."

"It's a trap," Hans repeated. "Eichmann plans to kill all the council members tonight."

Stern frowned. "How do you know about this?" he asked. "Who are you?"

"Wallenberg sent me," Hans replied. "My name is Hans Von Edler."

"Wallenberg, eh?" The old man nodded thoughtfully. "Wallenberg is a good man and can be trusted. He has proven himself to my people. If Wallenberg says is it so, it is so."

He turned and called, "Mama, come here quickly. We must go into hiding."

"You must hurry, sir," Hans urged. "Wallenberg says that if you and the other council members do not show up tonight, Eichmann's men will hunt you down. You and your family must go into hiding immediately."

Samu Stern nodded. "We will leave now, Hans. Is someone warning the others?"

"Ja," Hans replied, "Miklös Toth and I are telling all the council members. The only one I have not been able to warn is Dr. Peto. He was not at home."

The Jewish man pulled a watch from his pocket and glanced at it, frowning as he did so. "Nine o'clock is only half an hour away. Dr. Peto may be on his way to the council headquarters right now, and he'll walk right into Eichmann's trap. There isn't time to warn him."

He thought for a moment. "Son, would you run to the porter's lodge and tell Jakob Takacs to warn Dr. Peto if he comes? Ask Jakob to wait at the council headquarters."

Hans nodded. "I'm on my way."

The elderly Jew smiled. "God's blessings be upon you, lad."

Hans ducked into an underground tunnel behind Stern's house and raced back to the ghetto. He emerged from a manhole less than a block from the council headquarters. Keeping a sharp lookout for Arrow Cross *Nyalis,* he hurried to the porter's lodge. As he passed beneath a streetlight, he glanced at his watch. Ten minutes till nine.

A middle-aged man answered the door at Hans's insistent knock. "Are you Jakob Takacs?" Hans asked breathlessly.

The man nodded, glancing nervously up and down the street as he did. "Who's wanting to know?"

"You have to warn Dr. Peto!" Hans blurted. "Eichmann is planning to kill all the members of the Jewish Council tonight when they come to the meeting he has ordered. I couldn't find Dr. Peto, and you have to warn him."

The man held up both hands. "Slow down," he said. "What's this all about?"

"Eichmann called a meeting of the Jewish Council tonight at nine o'clock," Hans explained, "but Wallenberg learned that the colonel is planning to kill them all. Miklös Toth and I are warning all the council members, but I couldn't find Dr. Erno Peto. Herr Stern wants you to wait at the council headquarters and warn Dr. Peto when he comes."

"What time is it now?"

Hans pulled his watch from his pocket. "Eight minutes till nine."

"Then there's no time to lose. Peto is always punctual." Jakob Takacs stepped onto the porch without taking the time to grab a coat. "Come with me."

Hans hurried across the darkened street to the Jewish Council headquarters. As they reached the building, a tall man approached from the opposite direction. Takacs ran to meet him. "Erno, it's a trap," he said. "Eichmann is planning to kill you. Go into hiding!"

Without a word, the tall man turned and hurried away into the darkness.

Takacs looked at Hans. "Let's get back to the house, shall we? I'm about to freeze to death."

Back inside the lodge, Jakob Takacs hurried to the blazing fireplace. "Wait just a moment until I warm up again, will you?" he said to Hans. "I want to give you a message to take back to Wallenberg for me."

Hans nodded. "Sure."

Moments later, as Jakob stood at the counter hastily scribbling a note, three cars roared up in front of the lodge. Jakob looked up in alarm. "Hans," he said urgently, "get under the counter. Quickly!" Hans dropped to a hiding place beneath the counter. Moments later, the front door flew open and several Nazi officers stormed into the room. Hans heard a loud thud as one of the officers slapped his hand down angrily on the countertop, cursing as he did.

"Colonel Eichmann," Takacs greeted the man. "What a surprise to see you."

Eichmann! Hans began to tremble.

"Where are the Jewish Council members?" Eichmann screamed.

Hans could see Takacs's face, and the man looked puzzled and scared. "The council members?" he stammered. "I was told to have them here at nine o'clock tomorrow morning."

Eichmann was enraged. "Tonight!" he screamed. "They were to be here tonight!"

The porter backed away from the counter. Fear was written across his face. "I'm sorry, Colonel," he faltered, "but apparently there has been a misunderstanding. I apologize for the mix-up."

"Get them here at once!" Eichmann screamed. Jakob's sister came running into the room to see what was wrong, and the Nazi colonel noticed her arrival. "If the council members are not here in five minutes, I'll shoot you! And your sister!"

"Five minutes?" Jakob echoed. "But, Colonel, that would be impossible. They were told to assemble tomorrow morning. Who knows where they are now? Who could find them at this hour of the night?"

One of Eichmann's aides stepped forward and struck the porter over the head with his pistol. He continued to lash out until Jakob fell bleeding to the floor.

The Nazi colonel turned to the man's sister. "When your brother wakes up, tell him I expect the entire Jewish Council to be assembled right here at nine tomorrow morning. If they are not, I will shoot you and your brother. I give you my word."

The Nazis hurried to their cars.

Hans waited just a few seconds and then crawled from beneath the counter. He knelt beside the woman, who was bent over her brother. "I'll go to Wallenberg and ask for a doctor."

Jakob's sister grabbed Hans's arm. "No. I am a nurse, and I will look after Jakob. He will be all right. We must not endanger anyone else."

She glanced fearfully toward the door. "Go quickly. You must not be here if Eichmann returns. We will be fine."

"So anyway, the council members all assembled at nine o'clock this morning," Miklös told Hans as they traveled underground toward Wallenberg's office, "knowing that they were forfeiting their own lives by doing so."

Hans swung his flashlight beam in Miklös' direction. "Why did they do that?" he interrupted. "We warned them about what was going to happen!" He shook his head sadly. "Why didn't they listen?"

"Get your light out of my face," Miklös replied. "I can't see a thing."

"Sorry." Hans directed his flashlight beam toward the floor of the sewer tunnel.

"The council members obeyed Eichmann because they knew that other innocent people would die if they didn't," Miklös continued. "But wait till you hear what happened. They waited in fear for over two hours, expecting Eichmann to walk in at any minute and shoot them. Finally, a messenger came and told them that Eichmann and his men fled Budapest last night. There was only one road still open, and they took it."

Hans laughed. "Then we saved the council members' lives by warning them last night."

Miklös gave a little leap in the air. "We sure did. All the council members would have been killed last night if they had showed up when Eichmann wanted them to."

Hans was thoughtful. "I almost quit helping you and Wallenberg," he said quietly. "But if I had quit, some of those men might have died last night."

"I'm glad you didn't quit," Miklös replied.

Hans sighed. "God will give me the strength to keep serving, especially since I know Gretchen is in heaven."

Miklös nodded in agreement. "Of course. Gretchen was a good person."

Hans shook his head. "She's not in heaven because she was good, Miklös," Hans said seriously, praying as he realized that he had an opportunity to witness. "Gretchen is in heaven because she was a Christian and had her sins forgiven."

"Then are the sins of all Christians forgiven," Miklös asked, "even the Nazi Christians?" Hans tried to determine if the Jewish boy was serious or simply mocking him.

"You're still thinking of everyone as being either a Jew or a Christian," Hans replied. "But the Bible teaches that a Christian is someone who has received Jesus Christ as his personal Savior. Gretchen is in heaven because she had received Jesus."

"How does a person do that?" Miklös wanted to know.

"First, you must admit to God that you are a sinner," Hans answered, "and ask Him to forgive you for your sins. The Bible says: 'For all have sinned, and come short of the glory of God.' That's why none of us deserve heaven."

The boys turned a corner in the tunnel as they talked, and Hans stole a glance at Miklös. The Jewish boy appeared to be listening intently.

"Then you have to believe that Jesus is the Son of God, that He died for you on the cross, and that He rose from the grave the third day. The Bible tells us: 'But God commendeth His love toward us, in that, while we were yet sinners, Christ died for us.' "

Miklös cleared his throat. "My people keep the Law of Moses," he retorted, "given to us at Mount Sinai."

"Jesus kept the Law of Moses perfectly," Hans replied, "but He is the only one who ever has in all of history. He died for our sins because all of us have broken God's laws. That's what sin is."

Miklös was silent.

"If you believe that you are a sinner, and that Jesus died for you and rose again, then you need to ask Him by faith to be your Savior and forgive your sins. The Bible says: 'But as many as received Him, to them gave He power to become the sons of God, even to them that believe on His name.' "

Hans turned his light in Miklös's direction and looked at him. "Miklös, wouldn't you like to ask Jesus Christ to save you, like Gretchen and I have done? He wants to forgive your sins if you'll just ask Him."

Miklös shook his head. "I'll have to think about that for a while."

"Well, just remember that according to the Bible, good deeds won't take us to heaven, and religion won't take us to heaven. You need Jesus to save you. Gretchen is in heaven today because one day she asked Him to save her. You can do the same thing."

Miklös dropped his head and began to walk faster.

Moments later, Hans turned his flashlight on a makeshift ladder leading upwards. "Here we are. Let's check in with Madame Wohl and see if Wallenberg left us any new assignments."

The boys slipped into the office through the side door. Madame Wohl looked up as they entered. "Wallenberg," she called, "Hans is here!"

Wallenberg strode into the room, and Hans noticed a strange look on his face. "Hans! I'm glad you're here. We were just coming to get you." A look of delight swept across his face. "You won't believe the good news!"

Wallenberg turned and called, "Major! In here!" A tall, dignified Nazi officer hurried into the room, followed by a slender girl dressed in a filthy coat.

Hans stared, unable to believe his eyes. He ran forward. "Gretchen!"

CHAPTER NINETEEN

AN INCREDIBLE STORY

"Wait in the stairwell until I prepare Papa," Hans told Gretchen as Wallenberg's car rolled away from the curb. He opened the door to the apartment. A warm feeling of satisfaction swept over him as he watched his sister step inside. "Gretchen, it's good to have you home."

Gretchen hugged Hans for the tenth time, and her tears fell again on his shoulder. "I missed you, Hans. I was so afraid."

Hans blinked back tears of his own. He turned his head, suddenly embarrassed as his emotions overwhelmed him. "Whew," he said, trying to regain his composure, "you could use a bath!"

Gretchen took him seriously. "It's the first thing I'll do," she promised, "as soon as I see Papa."

Hans laughed. "I was teasing," he said. He hugged her again. "It's wonderful to have you home! Losing you was just as bad as losing Mama." He reached out and gently touched her face, almost as if he needed proof that she was actually standing before him. "I never thought I'd see you again till we got to heaven."

When they reached the top of the stairs Hans, whispered, "Wait here. I'll just take a second. Listen for my signal."

Hans stepped into the tiny apartment, not quite closing the door behind him. Papa was at the kitchen table slicing potatoes. Hans sat down across from him.

"Papa, if you could have any wish you wanted, what would you ask for?"

Papa looked up wearily. "Oh, I don't know, Hans," he replied. "What kind of a question is that?"

Hans shrugged, hardly able to contain his excitement. "Just name something, Papa."

Papa continued working on the potatoes. Many of them were rotting, and he was doing his best to remove the bad spots without sacrificing the tiniest bit of edible potato. "I wish that the war would be over soon," he said. "I wish that Eichmann would leave the Jews alone and that Gretchen . . ." Papa stopped, let the knife fall to the table, and dropped his head into his hands. His body shook with sobs.

Hans could wait no longer. "Papa," he said, "Gretchen is still alive."

Papa raised his head to look at Hans. "I wish it were true, Hans, I wish it were true."

At that moment, Gretchen slipped into the kitchen. "Papa!"

Papa stared at Gretchen. His eyes welled up with tears, and his lips moved as though he were speaking, but no sound came out. Finally, he simply held out his arms to her.

"Papa!" Gretchen fell into his arms, and the tears flowed freely.

"All right, Fraulein Gretchen," Papa said, shoving his plate to one side, "you've had your bath, and we've fed you. Now it's time to hear your story. How did you escape Auschwitz? We were told that all prisoners on the train had been gassed."

"God spared me," Gretchen replied as she began her story. Hans and Papa listened with tears in their eyes as Gretchen described her journey to Auschwitz. She told of the cattle car crowded with condemned Jews, of the hunger, the cold, and the terrible thirst. She told of the shock of realizing that some of her fellow travelers had died as the swaying train sped toward Auschwitz. Her father and brother wept as she described the loneliness and fear she experienced, knowing that each click of the train wheels brought her that much closer to a certain death.

As Gretchen described the death camp at Auschwitz, she broke into tears for the first time. "It was terrible, Papa," she sobbed. "They unloaded us from the cars, and everyone was crying. The guards marched us toward some big buildings that were supposed to look like shower houses, but we knew that they were . . ." Sobbing, she caught her breath, and then continued. "They were gas chambers."

The tears rolled down Gretchen's cheeks. "They marched a big group of the Jews into the buildings and then sealed the doors. The guards made the rest of us stand in the cold and wait for a long time, and we knew . . ." she cried harder. "We knew what was happening."

Hans could curb his impatience no longer. He had to ask the question. "How did you escape?"

"One of the Jewish men pulled out a fancy gold watch," Gretchen answered, "and showed it to one of the guards. I think he was trying to use it to bargain for his life. Anyway, some of the other guards saw the watch, and I guess it was really valuable, because several of them started fighting each other for it."

Gretchen wiped her eyes with the handkerchief Papa offered her. "I was toward the end of the line, and it was pretty dark. I noticed that we were standing right behind a big army truck, so when the fight started and everybody was yelling and running around, I just climbed over the tailgate of the truck and lay down. It was one of those trucks with a canvas cover over the back, you know, like they haul troops in."

"And nobody saw you?" Hans interrupted.

Gretchen shook her head. "*Nein,* I guess not."

Papa wiped his eyes with his handkerchief. "God was with you, sweetheart."

"I lay in the back of the truck," Gretchen continued, "while they took the rest of the people into the buildings. It was so cold! It was even colder than when we were on the train. After a while, the whole place got quiet, so I started planning to try to escape."

Hans leaned forward eagerly.

"When I raised up and looked over the tailgate of the truck, I could see that there was a barb wire fence around the whole camp. There were floodlights over the front gates, and I could see that the gates were chained and locked. Two soldiers with big dogs were patrolling back and forth, and I suddenly realized that I could never hope to escape.

"I lay down on the cold steel floor of the truck, and I guess I cried myself to sleep. The next thing I knew, I heard a rumbling noise, and the floor of the truck was shaking. Someone was driving the truck. I sat up and noticed that there was sunlight streaming in through the opening in the canvas at the back of the truck.

"When I peeked over the tailgate, the first thing I saw was pure white snow everywhere. I suppose it must have been snowing most of the night. But best of all, I could see no fences or buildings or trucks, just mountains and trees and snow! It was then that I realized that God had gotten me out of Auschwitz alive. I knelt on the floor of the bouncing truck and thanked God with all my heart."

Hans interrupted. "You know what I just thought of?" he said. "Herr Wallenberg didn't have anything to do with your rescue; it was God!"

He glanced at Papa and then back to Gretchen. "When we went to the brickyard, I thought that Wallenberg would be able to get you out. When he failed to save you from the train, I figured there was no hope for you. I guess I almost had more faith in Wallenberg than I did in God."

Papa nodded. "I guess we all learned something, didn't we?"

"I didn't know where the truck was going," Gretchen continued, "but I knew I had to get out somehow before it reached its destination. A few minutes later, the driver slowed down for a really tight hairpin curve. I would guess that the truck was doing less than thirty kilometers per hour. Anyway, when the truck made the turn, I climbed out on the back and jumped as far as I could to the side of the road. I landed in a deep snowdrift, so I wasn't even hurt."

Gretchen poured herself a glass of water and drank it without stopping for a breath. "The first thing I did was to eat a little bit of snow because I was so thirsty. But I didn't eat very much because I know that people freeze to death that way. The next thing I did was get on my knees in the snow and thank God again for saving me from Auschwitz."

Gretchen's face broke into a huge smile. "When I got up from my knees, I saw a kind-looking man standing in the middle of the road, looking at me. 'Fraulein, are you lost?' he asked, and I said, '*Ja,* I've just escaped from Auschwitz, and I don't know where to go.'

" 'Follow me,' he said, and he helped me out of the snowdrift. He was speaking perfect German, and yet I could tell that he wasn't German. He had the kindest face I have ever seen. We started walking along the road, and I kept looking over my shoulder to watch out for more trucks. He noticed, and told me not to worry, since there would be no more vehicles until after we got where we were going."

Gretchen looked at her father. "Papa, do you know what that man did? He reached inside his coat and pulled out a one-liter bottle of milk! He pulled out the stopper and handed it to me. I drank the whole thing. Then he pulled out a boiled potato and gave it to me. Papa, it was still hot. I've never had anything that tasted so good!"

Hans glanced at Papa and saw that his eyes were filled with tears.

"We walked five or six kilometers down the road, but like the man said, no traffic came that whole time. Finally, the man stopped and pointed to a deserted farm a short distance from the road. 'Go to the barn,' he told me, 'and there will be people who will take care of you and help you get back to Budapest.' "

Gretchen suddenly paused, and a bewildered look passed over her features. "Papa, I never even told him I was from Budapest," she exclaimed. "How did he know?"

Papa shook his head. "I don't know, sweetheart," he replied with a puzzled frown. "What happened next?"

"Well, I thanked the man and started across the field through the snow," Gretchen replied. "While I was with that man, I felt very safe and very happy. But when I had taken just a few steps in the field, I suddenly felt very alone and very afraid. I began to wonder what I should do if there was no one in the barn, so I turned around to ask my friend. Papa, he was gone! There was no one there!

"I ran back to the road to see where he could have gone, but he wasn't there. I looked both ways, but the roadway was empty, and there were no trees or bushes right there to hide him from my view. I could see my footprints in the snow leading into the field and back to the road again, but his footprints ended right there in the middle of the road!"

"An angel," Hans breathed. "He was an angel!"

Gretchen's eyes grew wide. "Papa, do you think he could have been? Did I really see an angel?"

Papa had a faraway look in his eyes. "I don't know, Gretchen," he answered slowly. "Maybe. The Book of Hebrews tells us that angels are ministering spirits, and this man did minister to you, didn't he?"

Gretchen nodded. "*Ja*. I guess he saved my life."

Hans leaned forward again. "What kind of clothes was he wearing?"

Gretchen thought for a moment. "I guess I didn't really notice," she answered slowly.

"So what happened next?" Hans asked.

"Well, I crossed the field to the farm," Gretchen continued, "and three trucks came by while I was going. I dropped down in the snow each time so they wouldn't see me. When I went inside the barn, it was empty. Some old, dusty hay was scattered around, but there was nothing else. The barn looked like it was falling down.

"I stood in the middle and called out, 'Is anybody here? I need help!' To my astonishment, a man stepped out of one of the empty cattle stalls a moment later!"

"Where did he come from?" Hans asked.

"There were eighteen Jews hiding in a secret room below the barn," Gretchen replied. "There was a tunnel leading down to a room about four meters wide and five meters long. One of the men had dug it two years ago, before most people even knew what the Nazis were doing to the Jews. There were eight adults and ten children, and I was the only person who was not a Jew."

Gretchen yawned and rubbed her eyes. "I'm so tired," she said.

Papa laughed. "Your bed is right where you left it three weeks ago."

"Finish the story first," Hans begged.

Gretchen shrugged. "There isn't much more to tell," she answered. "I stayed with them for nearly two weeks. We had cabbage and potatoes, which a loyal Gentile friend delivered every three days. When he found out that I was from Budapest and had helped Wallenberg, he told me that he knew how to get me back home. Two days later, he showed up with the Nazi major that you saw at Wallenberg's office."

"Who is the major," Hans asked, "and why did he help you? Is he really a Nazi officer?"

"His name is Major Seidel," Gretchen replied sleepily, "and he is really a Nazi officer, but he says he got tired of all the killing and became a double agent for the Allies. I think he's one of Wallenberg's informants. Anyway, I rode back to Budapest under some blankets in the trunk of his automobile."

Gretchen looked at Hans. "So that's my whole story. I thought I was going to die at Auschwitz, but the Lord saved me from it."

Papa fell to his knees beside Gretchen's chair. Placing one hand on her arm, he bowed his head and began to pray. Hans slipped from his chair and knelt beside him. "My gracious Father," Papa prayed, "when I lost my little girl three weeks ago, I never thought I would see her again this side of heaven. Thank You, Father, for being so merciful to return her to us again. Our hearts are full of praise to Your name for Your goodness to us!"

Papa prayed for nearly ten minutes, pouring out his gratitude for Gretchen's safe return. Hans felt as if his own heart would burst with happiness as he listened to his father pray. God had been gracious to them!

Papa finished praying, and Hans opened his eyes. He laughed at what he saw. Gretchen was fast asleep. Her head had fallen over and was leaning against the top of Papa's head for support.

Hans stood to his feet. He gently lifted Gretchen from her chair and carried her to the other room, being careful not to wake her as he lowered her into her bed. "Sleep well, Gretchen," he whispered, "and welcome home."

CHAPTER TWENTY
THE FINAL CONFRONTATION

"You won't believe who came to see Wallenberg yesterday," Miklös told Hans and Gretchen as they hurried through a dank corridor toward Wallenberg's Ulloi Street office. "Pal Szalai!"

Hans swept his light in Miklös's direction and stared at his friend. "Szalai? The Arrow Cross officer?"

Miklös nodded. "Right."

"What did he want?" Gretchen asked.

"Believe it or not," Miklös answered, "he wants to help us. He says he's tired of all the killing, and he wants to help Wallenberg rescue the Jews."

"Oh sure," Hans muttered. "He's probably just setting a trap for Wallenberg."

"I don't think so," Miklös replied. "Szalai provided Wallenberg with bodyguards, and he's stationed guards around the perimeter of the ghetto to stop Arrow Cross raids. You know how good Wallenberg is at sizing up people, right? Well, he says that he thinks Szalai is telling the truth and really wants to help us."

Hans shook his head. "It's still hard to believe."

The last, dark days of December seemed to stretch on and on. The residents of Budapest had grown weary of the constant sound of gunfire, artillery shells, and exploding bombs. The Russian army was so close that often the soldiers were visible to the residents of Budapest, but the German Nazis and the Hungarian Arrow Cross still controlled the city.

General August Schmidthuber, the highest-ranking Nazi in Budapest, had orders to hold Budapest until the last Nazi was dead. He also had orders to make sure that every Jew was killed before the Russians took the city. There were thirty-five thousand Jews living in protected houses and seventy thousand more in the Central Ghetto. Wallenberg and his staff knew that they were in a race against time as they fought to keep the Jews alive until the Russians came.

Pal Szalai was as good as his word. He kept Wallenberg and the legation staff informed of the activities of the SS and the Arrow Cross, and on occasion, even provided bodyguards and troops to help in some of the rescues. One snowy day in January, he proved his loyalties once and for all.

Hans and Miklös had finished a delivery of medicine to a safe house in the vicinity of town hall and were dashing back to the manhole in an alley when a passing automobile suddenly pulled over to the curb. "Boys," a voice called from the passenger's window, "I need your help." Miklös and Hans approached the vehicle warily.

The man in the car was Pal Szalai. "You're some of Wallenberg's boys, aren't you?" he said hurriedly. "I believe I've seen you at his Ulloi Street office."

Miklös nodded. "We serve as couriers for him."

"Get word to Wallenberg as fast as you can," Szalai told them. "The pogrom is about to start. Five hundred SS soldiers and twenty-two Arrow Cross troops are at the Royal Hotel right now, and they're requesting two hundred of our Hungarian police. The firing squads are going to kill everyone in the ghetto. Tell Wallenberg that I'm going right to Vajna."

Fifteen minutes later, Hans and Miklös breathlessly told the story to Wallenberg. "So, they're going to kill all the Jews," Miklös blurted. "Szalai is going to Vajna to try to get him to stop it."

A look of pain and sorrow crossed the diplomat's face. "Then it's finally happening," he said quietly. "This is the day we've been working against."

He grabbed his coat and a fur hat. "Vilmos!" he shouted, "hurry. This is our most important mission ever."

Tires squealed on the pavement as Wallenberg's Packard turned the corner at Attila Avenue. Vilmos braked to a screeching stop in front of the office of the Ministry of the Interior. "Stay here," Wallenberg told Hans and Miklös and then leaped from the car. At that moment, another car arrived from the opposite direction.

The man who jumped out was Pal Szalai. Together, the two men rushed into the building. Realizing what was at stake, Hans bowed his head and began to pray.

Ten minutes later, Wallenberg and Szalai exited the building. Vilmos rolled down the window. "Vajna wouldn't listen," Wallenberg told Vilmos in defeat. "He doesn't care about anything anymore, not even saving his own skin. He refused to stop the pogrom."

"There's only one man that can help us now," Szalai said.

Wallenberg looked up. "General Schmidthuber. Let's go see him."

Pal Szalai grabbed the sleeve of Wallenberg's coat. "Wait," he pleaded. "You can't go in person. He'd kill you immediately! Let me go. I'll use your name and tell him that you intend to hold him responsible if the Jews in the ghetto are killed. But if you go into his office, he'll have you killed, and then you're no longer a threat to him."

Wallenberg nodded. "I see your point." He stepped toward his car. "May God go with you. The lives of our Jewish friends depend on you."

Hans and Miklös waited anxiously with Wallenberg and his staff at the Ulloi Street office. Would Pal Szalai be successful in his attempt to persuade the SS general to cancel the massacre of the Jews in the ghetto? Seventy thousand lives were at stake.

It was nearly two o'clock when the messenger from Szalai slipped through the door. "Szalai gave General Schmidthuber your message," he told the anxious diplomat in front of the rest of the staff, "and the general called Vajna, Lucska from the Arrow Cross, and the head of the German garrison. When the men came to his office, he ordered them to cancel the pogrom."

Wallenberg dropped his head into his hands. "Thank God," he whispered. "This was our greatest rescue of all!"

During the second week of January 1945, the Soviet soldiers took the city of Budapest. They worked underground, using the city's system of cisterns, storm drains, and sewers to advance from house to house and from street to street. The German Nazis and Hungarian Arrow Cross were quickly routed.

On January 13, Wallenberg surrendered himself to the Russians, explaining who he was and asking for a meeting with Soviet marshall Malinovsky. Wallenberg wanted to make arrangements to help the more than one hundred thousand Jews who were left without food or the necessities of life. The Russians interrogated him for the next four days.

Hans and Gretchen were at the Ulloi Street office with Papa on January 17 when the familiar Packard pulled up to the curb, followed by a car filled with Russian officers. Raoul Wallenberg and Vilmos Langfelder climbed out of the Packard, and many of Wallenberg's staff hurried outside to greet them. "I've got permission to go to Debrecen to meet with Marshall Malinovsky," Wallenberg announced excitedly. "I'm not sure if I'm going as a guest or as a prisoner, but I hope to be back in a week. There's so much to do when I get back."

Just then, two elderly Jewish men walked by, free for the first time in ten months. Wallenberg noticed the yellow stars still stitched to their jackets. He turned to his staff. "Our mission was not in vain."

Wallenberg spent the next several minutes giving special instructions to the staff. He and Langfelder hurried back to the Packard, and the car pulled away from the curb. The Russian escort swung in behind it.

Miklös strode up to stand between Hans and Gretchen as they watched the Packard disappear down the street. "Raoul Wallenberg is the greatest man I ever met," the Jewish boy said softly. "He has the heart of a prince."

"Nein," Papa corrected, "not a prince. Wallenberg has the heart of a servant."

Epilogue

Hans, Gretchen, and Miklös are fictional characters, of course, but Raoul Wallenberg, Vilmos Langfelder, Tom Veres, Madame Wohl, and Lars Berg were real people. Incredibly, the rescues of Hungarian Jews described in this book actually took place.

Wallenberg arrived in Budapest on July 6, 1944, as the Second Secretary of the Swedish Legation. He started and organized Section C of the legation and soon had over four hundred Jews working determinedly to save the lives of other Jews. It has been estimated that Wallenberg and his staff were directly responsible for saving the lives of more than one hundred thousand people!

Those who knew Wallenberg are quick to testify that he had the heart of a servant. It seemed that he was willing to do anything to help the Jewish people, whether it was making a phone call to an important government official, finding milk powder for a young mother, or helping in a soup kitchen. During the most desperate days of the struggle to save Jewish lives, this brave diplomat worked twenty hours a day, sleeping less than four hours a night. Wallenberg lived to serve others.

His story ends on a sad note. After the Russians had captured Budapest, Wallenberg surrendered himself to the Russian commander. On January 17, 1945, Wallenberg and his chauffeur, Vilmos Langfelder, were driven from Budapest in their own car, escorted by a number of Russian officers. Neither man was ever seen again in the free world. Apparently, they spent the rest of their lives in a Soviet prison. Soviet prisoners released as late as 1975 insisted that Wallenberg was still alive as a Soviet prisoner. For Raoul Wallenberg, servanthood was costly.

In 1981, United States president Ronald Reagan signed legislation making Wallenberg an honorary U.S. citizen, an honor extended to just three other persons in all of history: Marquis de Lafayette, Sir Winston Churchill, and Mother Teresa. U.S. Senator Tom Lantos, a Hungarian Jew who had been rescued as a teenager by Wallenberg, sponsored the bill honoring Wallenberg. Lantos's wife, Annette, who also owed her life to Wallenberg, had this to say about this courageous, unselfish man:

> *He was like a Moses from the north, who came to us in the most terrible days. His noble and courageous deeds truly shone like a bright light in that abysmal darkness. Just remembering his goodness and his sacrifice for our sake, somehow helped to heal my own emotional and spiritual wounds.*

The story of Raoul Wallenberg is a story of humility, courage, and compassion. Here was a man with a servant's heart.

Glossary

danke schön (**dahn**·kuh shayn) many thanks

Einsatzkommando (**eyen**·sawtz·kommondo) special detail with particular assignment

Frau (frauw) Mrs.

Fräulein (**froy**·lyn) lady or Miss

Gendarmes (**jzahn**·darm) police

Gulyassuppe (**goo**·ea·**zoo**·peh) a stew or soup of Hungarian origin

gut (goot) good

guten tag (goot·uhn **tahg**) good day, how do you do?

Herr (Hehr) sir, Mr.

Ich bin (**Ick** bin) I am

ja (yah) yes

Judenfrei (**yoo**·den·fry) free of Jews

Knabe (**knah**·buh) boy

nein (nine) no

Nyalis (**nie**·al·is) Hungarian Nazis

Reich (righk) used with Third to denote the German power under Hitler

schnell machen (**shnell** mock·en) move faster, go

Schützpasse (**shurtz**·pauzzah) a protective passport

Schutzstaffel (**shurtz**·staf·el) elite protection squads. Abbreviation: SS

shalom (shah·**lohm**) Hebrew word for peace, a common greeting

Swastika (**svah**·stick·ah) entwined broken crosses